Inside Out

By

Patricia Toulson

This book is dedicated to Chris, Lynn, Jill, Heather and the radiographers from the 1960's to present day.

My grateful thanks to Jenny Scott who oversaw every stage with care to detail and much enthusiasm.

The medical cases recounted in this book are true.

However, places, names and some identifying characteristics have been changed.

The views expressed in this book are entirely those of the author.

Chapter 1

We always said you could count the trees on Clapham Common.

Yet even here adventures could happen, secret paths followed and dens made, for it was in this place that in the late summer of 1951, when I was 5 years old, a bizarre accident determined my future career.

Halfway across the green sward was a large murky pond, where we fished with sixpenny nets on bamboo canes for tiddlers, transferring any precious catch to a string handled jam-jar along with a sprig of dark green weed immersed in smelly, bitty water. Here we sailed James' small wooden yacht with its two white cotton sails, pulled along by a length of twine in case his wonderful birthday present from Granny floated out too far or heaven forbid sank. And it was here that we came for the last picnic of that summer.

The picnic was over so while our mother packed everything away James and I played chase just beyond the pond where there was a steep slope, supporting several of the few substantial trees. James, who was four years older than me, darted expertly in and out of their stiff, wide trunks closing fast the gap between us. In my excitement to escape my brother's clutches, I ran too fast down the incline, pitching forward over unsteady chubby legs and then calamitously thrust my chin, full force, into the harsh bark of one these very few measurable trees!

I can't recall the journey to the casualty department of the famous St Thomas's Hospital in South London that followed, but I vividly remember being taken down, to the typically placed basement x-ray department of the hospital, where great water pipes ran the lengths of those deep sited corridors, for a series of jaw x-rays. Two lovely ladies, radiographers, in gleaming, white dresses with bright red belts adorning their waists, then twisted and turned my head in all sorts of unusual ways to get the pictures they wanted. I was fascinated.

They, of course, were delighted that instead of screams of fear I wanted to know what was happening, wondering how they could see what was inside my face. I tried very hard to keep as still as possible, determinedly obeying their instructions, but for them, keeping me from asking questions was much harder. As a treat for my good behaviour they rewarded me with a tour of the "wet room", a well-lit area where the x-ray films came out of the darkroom to be viewed and washed ready for drying. I never forgot the peculiar smell of chemicals being washed off in large water tanks, while large and small dripping black and white shiny sheets were being held up for inspection against special light boxes. It was all very mysterious and thrilling; I wanted to look like those pretty ladies wearing white dresses with their red belts nipping in their waists and take magic pictures that saw right inside you.

Now, today, it was 8.40 am on the first Monday in September 1962 just as that future was about to begin.

This was the first time a new school term was of no importance to me, instead an unknown journey, a new life, could just be waiting for me across the street. There, on the opposite side, stood an imposing, grey stone building, its three storeys of multi-paned, white-framed windows portraying an elegant Georgian façade. Four white central columns, two either side framed the deep blue entrance doors. That autumnal morning, sunlight flickered across the glazing giving it a pleasing sparkle, lifting my spirits.

I took a long look before I made what struck me as "symbolic" footsteps crossing to the other side. Would this prove to be a decisive move forward in my life?

Today, at sixteen years of age, I realised my childhood would be left behind once I stepped beyond those imposing double doors.

My heart skipped beats in nervous anticipation whilst I stood looking up at the stone portico plinth above the entrance, engraved with the name, "Elmbridge General Hospital".

"Now then girls! Shoulders back, head high," rang the voice of our deportment mistress, Miss James, her words echoing in my head.

"Pride in your school and yourselves at all times, carry yourselves well, keep your back straight however tall you are!!," she insisted, eyes directed firmly at my gangly hunched, frame; dignified posture had been of great importance at Meadway County Grammar School. I drew myself more erect, acknowledging that in spite of our embarrassed giggles she had of course been right.

Once before, I had crossed this threshold to attend an interview at the hospital, but such was my state of panic that day I had scarcely taken in any of my surroundings.

A large blue arrowed sign, pointed the way to the X-ray Department along a sloping corridor. I vaguely remembered from attending for interview, the strange heavy plastic doors, which seemed to clap enthusiastically in approval once the struggle to pass through them, had been tested and won.

Reluctantly, these thick opalescent flaps gave way to wheel chair pushers when empty but almost always tried to consume any chair that carried a passenger, especially if an outstretched leg covered in plaster of Paris tried to brazen its wearer through. Some long time later I learned the trick to turn the chair round and sneak it through backwards. However strong gusts of wind had no problem in entering, in fact the doors invited them in, causing a permanent draught to sweep along the chain of corridors. On this my first official day I plunged determinedly through them causing them to flap loudly and announce my passage to everyone.

Wearing the prescribed sensible shoes, I clapped down the wooden floored passage until reaching the dead-end that was the X-ray department. I discovered over the years that X-ray departments were either in the bowels of hospitals or in the least accessible location. It would appear that Hospital planners seemed to fear these "magical" rays, placing departments full of alien equipment, into areas where they could be avoided as much as possible.

At the end of the corridor, leaning against the X-ray department reception desk stood a large, grey haired man, clad in a tightly fitting brown overall, buttons straining ready to pop at his first laugh, sneeze or cough. "Well young miss can I help you?" he asked cheerily.

His brown eyes smiled warmly at me as I replied, trying to produce a confident voice, "Oh! I've come to work here."

"No, no young miss, you must have got that wrong, we don't work here do we Mrs Lewis?"

"Stop teasing Ted, you've got her all worried!" she chided, seeing my cheeks begin to turn uncomfortably pink. Come here luv, you must be our new cadet nurse. Come on round the back and have a quick cuppa before sister comes."

She put a friendly arm around me and steered me through small gaps between cabinet after cabinet of thick paper envelopes, splitting and scuffed by their shiny contents, into a back room where the kettle was whistling away on a blue flamed gas ring.

Mrs Lewis was dressed in a lilac-striped uniform with a white starched cap perched on her fluffy grey speckled hair, where it sat slightly "drunkenly" to one side, held on by white painted hair clips. Around her waist she wore a plain white belt, this uniform denoted her position as a Nursing Auxiliary. "We've got five minutes before Sister comes then we have to move sharpish! What's your name luv?" she asked as she lit the remaining half of a cigarette and drew the smoke in with a relish.

"Mary. What's Sister like?" I asked feeling much more at ease with this motherly figure, "I only met Dr. Hugo when I came for interview, he was really nice,"

"Well she can be a bit fierce but not to worry, we'll see you're all right. Oh! God here she comes, quick get back out the front with Ted while I stub me fag out!" she waved her arms about trying ineffectually to disperse the smoke through a tiny open window.

Then, for the first time of many, I heard the small rapid, tripping footsteps coming down the wooden floored corridor, thankfully giving an early warning of the approaching Sister.

How is it possible to describe the effect she had on this sixteen year old, straight from school?

Well firstly, she was five feet nothing, tiny beside my gangling thin frame of five feet eight inches. Next she was dressed in a crisp, white coat with blue epaulets; its sleeves tightly ringed by white starched cuffs, encircled around her miniscule waist sat a blue stiff, silver buckled belt, denoting her superior status. She wore black stockings with her dainty feet encased in black lace up shoes, whose square raised heels added a small but vital lift to her stature. Finally on her head sat, perfectly centred, a frilly starched cap, which dared not move, even as she peered up to me with a very stern face.

With a disdainful look her shrewd eyes measured me from head to toe. Instinctively I shrunk back waiting for the barbed comment that was surely to follow.

"If you are the new nursing cadet I will not speak to you again until you are properly attired," she snapped and with that she tripped away, heels clicking her path to the Superintendent Radiographer's office, shutting the door firmly behind her.

I stood shaking in her wake, I was twice her size and terrified.

"Don't look so scared deary, I'll take you to the nurses home where they will kit you out," chuckled Ted, "She snaps like a terrier does that one, especially if you're bigger than her

They say she has a good heart under it all!"

It was many, weeks before I could find any minute sliver of a heart in Sister Aster.

I had left school, aged sixteen, achieving a reasonable seven passes in my GCE exams, including Maths and two science subjects. These were the required entry qualifications to become a student radiographer, Radiography being the career path I aspired to follow. Unfortunately as I was only sixteen, I couldn't start training until at the earliest, October 1963 so my parents & I thought if I could gain some experience as a cadet nurse, attached to an X-ray department, it would be of great benefit. My headmistress had disagreed, claiming two further years of education in a sixth form, to achieve A level passes, would be of much better use to my future.

Ignoring her advice I contacted Elmbridge General Hospital, where to my delight the recruitment people were happy to employ me as a specialised, cadet nurse attached permanently to the x-ray department. Luckily a new School of Radiography was planned to open in the autumn of 1962. This new, rather experimental venture was in conjunction with another larger hospital, Brunswick General, 20 miles away, where academic training would take place once a week leaving practical tuition within each hospital's own department. Thus a joint possible in-take of 10 students would make this a financially viable prospect, with the expectation that both hospitals would gain prestige and recognition of their training school status.

Now, this was my first day towards that goal. Ted led me over to the adjoining Nurses Home to be clothed in an official hospital uniform. I was very excited.

He left me in the charge of Home Sister, whose whole life was devoted to the care and frustration of managing blossoming young women and trying to turn them into well disciplined efficient nurses. This tall, weary faced woman with greying red hair, tendrils escaping the control of her cap, had an onerous task. A new spirit of independence was cascading through England's youth, who were at last free from the anxieties of war and the restrictions of rationing. Life to these student nurses promised to be exhilarating, free of many of the heavy responsibilities their parents had lived through. For them Home Sister's "Victorian - styled" rules were only there to be refuted, her chastisement to be shrugged off without remorse but to me that day she seemed all powerful. She opened the door to a small locker room, then after closely examining me through narrowed eyes, selected from a large pile a white button through dress, a stiff white belt and an even stiffer little white cap, which had two white painted hair-clips attached.

"This dress will do until you are properly measured and fitted for three of your own," she instructed sternly, "Meanwhile do not try to shorten this one. Wear your cap at all times. Do not run, shout, laugh or make any exhibition of yourself! This is a hospital, which is an institution to be respected at all times!" these words of command rang with emotional reverence, as she continued, "Your current nursing cadet status puts you directly under Matron's charge but as you are attached to x-ray, Sister Aster will see to your daily duties." She turned abruptly then swept out.

I hastily stripped off down to my underwear and pulled the cardboard starched, white dress over my head. With shaking fingers I struggled to manipulate slippery buttons into heavily starched button-holes and tried somehow to fix the silly little cap onto my freshly washed, iron-straight fair hair. The result was a white attired, white faced, gawky, revelation of virginity personified.

I made my way back to the department where Mrs. Lewis took one look at me, "Oh! My goodness is that supposed to fit you, " she exclaimed, "No way are you going to wear a dress suitable for someone sixteen stone when you are only about eight!"

"Well it was the only size long enough," I explained, "Home Sister said…"

"Come with me young Mary we are off to the sewing room" announced Mrs. Lewis and with that I was marched out of the department, along many corridors and up to the remotest part of the hospital high above the wards, then up a further flight of rickety stairs into the attic. Within this small room, hidden in the roof space, sat three nimble-fingered, podgy ladies, each peering round their sewing machines at this intrusion, they were the sole occupants of the sewing room. Probably most of the hospital staff was quite unaware that this place even existed. As I glanced around, my fertile imagination pictured the remote corner in Sleeping Beauty's castle, where the wicked witch kept her spinning wheel. Did these ladies keep some secret hidden away up here?

I was measured but chastised for being too thin. In 1962, pre-"Twiggy" years, thinness was not the shape women craved, Marilyn Monroe curves were aspired to, feminine, sexy, desirable. Sadly my flat-chested, bony frame with its protruding pelvic bones was sexless, boyish…how I longed to have a shapely bust (*breasts* was a term never referred to other than medically or maternally) to replace my meagre 32a cup bosom. However in spite of a healthy appetite and love of sweet things, skinny I was and skinny I stayed. I suppose these kindly ladies thought my bony figure was due to poor nutrition; anorexia was not a term in general use, it would have been completely foreign as a word or as a condition to these good women, anyway my dear Mum fed me well. She served our family a typically English diet of steak and kidney pie, suet pudding and treacle, lamb stew and dumplings with jam roly-poly and other unmentionable treats that today's life-style monitors would proclaim life-threatening! Duly measured and re-clad in my swathing ensemble allocated from Home Sister, we retraced our steps down to x-ray.

Within the week I was delivered three crisp white dresses which fitted me, even maintaining decency when I bent over. We cadet nurses were not given name badges as our status, the lowest of the nursing low, made it inconceivable anyone would want to know who we were.

Fortunately for both of us, another nursing cadet was attached to the nearby casualty and outpatients department. Her name was Anna and she already had several months' work experience to pass on to me. We soon became friends looking out for one another as best we could.

The sisters and senior nurses were hard task masters, needing only to look irritated for panic to well up in our throats. Anna told me she often hid in the x-ray linen cupboard, to cry out of sight, following some chastisement from one of the more spiteful staff-nurses. I vowed that whatever telling off, however unfair, I would not cry. Instead my tears of frustration and anger were to come at night alone in bed; never, ever did I spill tears to give any satisfaction to a bullying tormentor.

On this my first day, clad in this enormous white dress, which Mrs Lewis had tried to adjust with strategically placed safety pins, I reported back to Sister Aster.

"How well do you know your alphabet?" she questioned me with extreme seriousness as her heavily wrinkled brow rose to meet the lower edge of her cap.

"Very well of course," I replied rather indignantly, having been delighted to pass seven of the eight GCE exams I had taken in the summer.

"Then I expect the patient x-ray record cards to be filed exactly in alphabetical surname order," she said sternly, handing me a pile of index cards bearing hand written names in the top left hand corner. With that she tripped away her shoes tapping out the warning that she was on the move, only on this occasion just as far as her office, where she kept the door open enough to keep me in view. All morning I was to feel that piercing look darting menacingly my way.

Thinking this was my moment to impress, I began to stack the cards in order for ease of filing. Doctors, I knew, were re-known for the illegibility of their handwriting and at that moment I understood why this task was going to be more of a challenge than I had expected.

Fortunately our receptionist, Brenda, was an expert at unscrambling the scrawling patterns of ink purporting to be names and mostly, managed with great patience to transcribe them for me, however I faced another obstacle to this supposedly straightforward task.

A simple surname *Thompson* could be spelt *Tomson, Tompson* or*Thomson* so that when a patient had multiple cards their name had often been spelt in many different ways.

Which was correct? Who knows! I glanced around anxiously to seek advice and caught a triumphant glint in Sister Aster's eye as she peered across from her office desk in my direction. I might have thought I knew my alphabet but accurate filing was a different matter entirely. After half an hour she came to check my work. I stood back, heart thumping while she stood on tip-toe to peer into the A-B file drawer, her frilly capped head bobbing up and down. It didn't take her long to find an erroneously placed card.

"Aha!" she admonished triumphantly, "Allan with two Ls comes after Alan with one."

"I didn't file that card sister," I interrupted quickly.

"Well why did you not correct it," she retorted sharply, "take the whole file drawer out and sort them properly!" She pulled the drawer out to its maximum length then stepping back with one movement tugged it from its nest and smartly tipped all the cards upside down on to the neighbouring table with many tumbling to the floor. Wordlessly she turned smartly about and marched her tiny feet back to her office, this time closing the door firmly behind her.

I stood open-mouthed; I had never experienced anything or anyone quite like that before. "Never mind dearie," Mrs Lewis came quickly to my side, "I'll give you a hand to start," she said kindly as she bent to retrieve the debris. That one file took us until lunchtime and with sinking heart I realised that Sister Aster intended me to re-file the drawers all the way to Z...

There was one thing that kept me amused (while satisfying Sister Aster's need to restrict any enthusiasm I may have felt for my new position in her department), this was the extraordinary choices parents sometimes made for naming their offspring. To this day I well remember *Hazel Hazell, Leonard Leonard, George George & John Johns.*

Even with this light relief it was tedious toil. Any aspirations I may have had of working anywhere that involved actual patients, disappeared with the prospect of days of boring, menial, clerical duties.

That first day was a huge disappointment, in spite of the warmth and friendliness of Mrs. Lewis, Ted and the other ancillary staff.

Had my parents and I made the right decision? Perhaps, I reflected, joining a new sixth form, albeit in an unknown school, would have been the better option? Had I let Sister Aster manage to unsettle my ambitions? I became a child again, longing to go home and pour it all out to Mum, but home was still London, where my family had had to remain.

Mum and Dad had been due to move from South London to Elmbridge around the time I had started my duties at the hospital. Dad was taking early retirement from the Metropolitan Police Force as they happily realised the purchasing of our very own first home in the town in which my mother grew up (she was the youngest of nine children), and where many of her brothers and sisters still lived.

We had always lived in either rented or police accommodation, never being able to afford even the first rung on the ladder of home-ownership in London. Ironically it was only a few months after my father's retirement in 1962 that a serving police constable's pay increased to one thousand pounds per annum. Before this large increment happened even his inspector's wage had been meagre. All my childhood we had been "saving-up" for our own home, now at last the promised purchase was to be fulfilled. A contract had been signed for a newly completed semi-detached house with a sizable garden; their long awaited dream was coming true. Unfortunately, just three weeks before moving date, my older brother James contracted glandular fever and became very ill. He developed complications from this virus with encephalitis (inflammation around his brain) sending him urgently to hospital, where he struggled to fight its debilitating effects. My parents could not leave him so I had been sent to stay with one of my mother's sisters in a village outside Elmbridge. My aunt was a carefree lady, a hopeless cook with a ready laugh that brushed life's problems away. I knew she would "chivvy" me up but I was feeling too sorry for myself to put this difficult day into perspective. I was so worried about James, I worshipped my big brother and desperately needed to know how he was, but, without any house telephone, regular communication was impossible as the only telephone available was sited half-a-mile away on the village green; all of this added to my sorry state.

I felt overwhelmed with the strangeness of my new job, coping with Sister Aster's harshness and James' illness, although my aunt was very caring I felt very isolated from what was happening at home.

I knew I couldn't give my parents any extra worries so I resolved that night, that I would not let Sister Aster's best efforts to destroy my confidence succeed. She was not coming between me and my childhood dream. She was only my first obstacle, there would no doubt be countless more, so I resolved to learn as much as I could about my new environment and how best to fit in with the people who worked there.

Chapter 2

It was during my third week that I at last caught a tiny glimpse of "the good heart" in Sister Aster, which Ted had mentioned on my first day.

"Mary, I want to see you in my office now!" ordered the dreaded voice from Sister's office as I crept passed to the staff room for my morning break. My heart sank and with heavy legs I made my way over through her door.

"Close the door," she commanded "Sit down and don't fidget!"

Now what had I done! Nothing obvious came to mind but something must have upset her. Then suddenly as she looked across at me, the semblance of a smile transformed her usually irritated expression into a softness I had never seen before.

"I understand that your brother is unwell and in St. James' Hospital. You will take tomorrow off, catch the train to London and visit him. That's all, now go straight back and finish the filing you were doing before your break."

I sat there stunned for a moment, how had she learned of my family situation? I suspected Mrs. Lewis, had divulged the circumstances to her, being concerned to see me struggling with

Sister's attitude, as Mrs L. had taken me under her motherly wing. Sister Aster's sudden kindness had been so unexpected that it brought me closer to tears than any of her usual admonishing had done. "Go on, off with you!" she said gruffly. "Thank you Sister," I managed to reply then rushed out to tell Mrs. L. the good news.

Mrs L. beamed back at me, "She isn't all harshness you know but better get straight on with that filing, I think it's safer to miss your cuppa." I nodded grabbing a fistful of record cards with a rare enthusiasm for the deadly boring task of filing.

The next morning my aunt & I took the now amazingly quick train journey to London; only very recently had the length of the ride shrunk, from one and a half hours to one hour ten minutes, following electrification of the main line. It was a damp, dismal day, which matched my anxious mood. I tried not to picture my big brother lying disconsolately alongside other very sick men; he hated anything remotely medical, diving out of the sitting room if I tuned in to "Your life in their hands" on the television. Apart from the usual sibling quarrels we were close; he looked out for me and I hero-worshipped him. The train sped along, swinging rhythmically from side to side as I sat quietly muttering, "Please, please let him be better."

A noisy, stuffy, underground journey took us the final distance to the south London hospital bed he occupied. To my surprise he was being nursed in a single- bedded room attached to the men's medical ward for his own protection, rather than the other way about. It appeared his immune system was too weak to combat any infections from neighbouring patients or their visitors.

I was now familiar with the smell and disciplined atmosphere of a hospital ward but my aunt looked decidedly uncomfortable. I took her hand as we were shown into his spartan room with its one small window overlooking a chain of rooftops escaping into the distance. He was sitting out of bed in a green flecked, high-backed armchair, his skin reflecting the tinge of the fabric.

"James, I can't believe you are up, that's brilliant!" I greeted him delightedly.

"I persuaded...... the nurses..... to set me free ....for your visit," he replied in a slow stilted voice, thinking hard before each utterance, "didn't wan...t you pulling..... rank on me now...

you're a medical p..professional," he finished breathing hard but with a beaming

smile. It seemed at last the encephalitis was easing and his blood count was reaching more acceptable figures as the virus slowly retreated from his body. We spent a happy hour with him, discovering that he was having to learn to walk again, which was not an easy task as his now thin, gangly frame of six feet three made co-ordination and balancing difficult. He was also suffering great lapses of concentration but the doctors were optimistic and felt confident he would make a complete recovery.

Our return journey took us back through the dark, cobalt blue night of early winter but now, my humour had returned enough to relate some amusing work experiences to my aunt. As I chatted on the lights of Elmbridge station suddenly appeared and the train slowed to a halt. Hastily we gathered our coats and emerged into the cold, misty evening.

The next day I duly reported James' progress to Sister Aster and she seemed relieved that our previous relationship could be resumed. No further "soft-touch" was required, but now that I had discovered there was a caring heart beating in her diminutive chest,

I became less panicky around her and consequently made fewer mistakes. At last I was settling down, taking on a role as a useful "go-for" within the department, also now able to help out dear Mrs. L. and especially Stella with their duties.

This x-ray department was typical of those situated in small to middle sized hospitals in 1962. Here, there were three actual x-ray rooms, each lead-lined so that no x-rays could escape beyond the walls. Each room bristled with ominous looking machinery. Great grey metallic boxes stood in their corners full of oil, in which submerged transforming valves, were kept cool; their huge, heavy, black wrapped, power cables climbed across the ceilings to latch on to the x-ray tubes feeding them the energy to create penetrative x-rays. This electronic jungle of wires, cables, valves and of course the very precious x-ray tubes (the camera) were temperamental; breakdowns of equipment were frequent and frustrating.

Patients waited for their examinations in a long narrow corridor, linking the reception desk to the furthest room, Room 3. Busy clinic days had them spilling out into the general out-patients thorough-fare with wheelchairs and stretcher-trolleys vying for space. Those seated in the corridor could only gaze at a plain white tiled wall, which shielded the six changing cubicles from intrusive eyes, a necessary screen as nervous people often emerged with their examination gowns, fastened (where ties existed) at the front instead of the back, revealing rather more than anyone wanted to see!

One busy morning, Jeanette had asked me to get one of her patient's to change into an x-ray gown ready for his chest x-ray.

"Good morning Mr. Grant," I greeted him cheerfully as I led him to the changing cubicle, "Please undress to the waist only. If you are wearing any chains around your neck please remove them and put this gown on with the ties to the back," I handed him the crisp, white garment and he nodded in assent.

When Jeanette was ready for her next patient I knocked on the door of his cubicle, which opened quickly, revealing a short, barrel-chested man with a carpet of hair extending far beyond his waist to areas I was not expecting to see uncovered. He had removed every stitch of clothing, except his socks, (well, that's an Englishman's fetish) and to my horror stood smiling triumphantly with his gown on the wrong way round, flapping wide open, displaying his rather large, purple-tinged, stiff appendage pointing in my direction. I looked aghast as his hot heavy breath scorched my face and to my fury and humiliation, my cheeks burned crimson. I turned and fled to Jeanette who was checking films in the wet viewing room. My embarrassment was compounded further as everyone greeted my garbled tale with great hilarity, except Jeanette, who, beside herself with anger, marched to his cubicle and stood authoritively in front of the exposed Mr. Grant.

In a scornful command she ordered him, "Follow the instructions that were clearly given to you immediately, before I notify the authorities!" He shrank in size in all directions as he reversed the gown, suffering Jeanette's withering, disgusted, demeanour, which continued throughout his examination. His record card was duly marked and his GP would be informed. Mr. Grant would be unlikely to try that trick again, well not here anyway.

That experience had shaken me and for many weeks a packed corridor filled me with dread; my cheeks would burn as I hurried passed, eyes cast down praying no one would speak to me or even worse ask a question I couldn't possibly answer!

Between Rooms 2 and 3 and behind the changing cubicles sat the hub of the department, the wet-viewing room with its adjoining

Darkroom, which bore a sniggering reputation as the rendezvous for any out-of-hours romantic assignations.

In 1962 all x-ray films were processed by hand, a skill I would have to learn very quickly if I was going to be of any use at all. The distinctive smell from the developing chemicals, that I had remembered from my childhood permeated throughout the department helping to mask salacious smoking, which frequently took place in the wet room by radiographers, outpatient nurses or anybody who craved a quick "drag" while on duty.

The department's essential darkroom technician, Stuart, spent much of his working life devoid of light or fresh-air closeted in the darkroom and wet viewing areas. Although he had only just reached twenty, Stuart had honed his skills so efficiently that radiographers relied on his ability to judge the development of a film (called "watching") during its progression within the deeply darkened, closeted darkroom. These were radiographs taken in trying circumstances, where "first-time right" was the only option. They were often cases of urgent portable films rushed back from SCBU (Special Care Baby Unit), pregnancy films, where a mother was already far gone in labour, along with many other life threatening situations. A quiet, thoughtful lad, this skill made him a much valued member of the department and treated with respect by everyone.

It was a hot, noisy environment as the metal drying cabinet belted hot air around row upon row of shiny black and white negatives of all sizes. Annoyingly it proved to be a cupboard of trouble for me. However I hung the wet films, in whichever order of size or degree of wetness or dryness, I never satisfied the constant inspections of Sister Aster, who hovered anxiously around me, wasp-like, as I followed Stuart's instructions to load a fresh batch of dripping films into the drier. I prayed she would be called away to the telephone, before I made some silly mistake, knowing it would be followed by the sting of her sharp tongue but my prayer was ignored.

"For heaven sake cadet nurse can't you see the films will stick together if you place them like this? Wet films go on the bottom so they do not drip on the nearly dry ones, common sense girl that's all I ask, common sense!"

Her continued irritation at my incompetence never seem to abate, "I have never encountered anyone who could take so long and move so slowly in my entire career," she snapped through thin lips, then being unable to find any other fault with my performance she turned about and tripped off, her heels hammering out an irritated beat of tiny footsteps on the wooden floor, all the way back to her office.

 The three x-ray rooms had different, specialised functions, though all three could be used for general x-ray work. On the other side of the department beside the reception desk was a smaller waiting area especially for patients awaiting an examination in Room 1, the screening room. These people were usually very nervous, their only concern was how to get through the next two or three anxious hours, for one of their biggest concerns was gaining access to the two patient loos, thoughtfully situated close by.

The 'Screening Room' was where the more messy work of Barium meals and enemas took place. These examinations outlined the digestive system where fluid barium was either administered by mouth, "top down" or through a tube inserted into the anus, "bottom up;" hence the nervousness of the waiting victims. Other 'nasties' happened in there, some of which must have been dreamt up by a practical joker with a slightly sadistic bent.

Here was the domain of the three radiologists and a totally, unqualified screening technician, Letitia. More of her later, but first the three "deities," who ruled over everyone!

At Elmbridge Hospital there were three such doctors in charge of the X-ray department, they were the most senior staff, at the pinnacle of their careers, never to be crossed and always obeyed, except by Sister Aster of course, who manipulated them well. They were each always anxious to please her so that her support could be counted on in all inter-departmental politics; for these three men rarely agreed on anything!

It was wonderful to behold her on tip-toe, admonishing them in full flow as if they were mere medical students.

Dr. Aubrey Weston–Smythe was the Head of the Department, performing specialist procedures and reporting on a percentage of the day's radiographic out-put; he could even be interrupted by visiting clinicians or brave radiographers for advice. Dr. Weston-Smythe was a tall, elegant man with soft brown hair curling around his ears. He spent much of his time in his office only touring the department on a weekly basis, offering a benign word here and there, then, having made his obligatory appearance, retreated once more from sight. He also had a lucrative private practice with x-ray equipment installed into his very large, architect designed house. As his wife was a fully qualified radiographer, competent dark room technician and charming receptionist, his own skills ensured their Private Practice was complete. No wonder the expression he wore as he glided into and out of his office and around the department on his weekly tours had an "other worldly" air, which always seemed a trifle smug, but even he could be brought to earth by Sister Aster. Tiny as she was he would resort to any means to placate whatever had agitated this little firebrand.

Dr. Hugo would never have dreamt of working in the private field, all knew of his left-wing politics and quick temper; his secretary would deflect any unsuitable private requests to spare everyone the entire tirade that would surely follow.

He carried the heaviest workload, especially in the screening room where his God-like presence was enhanced by the huge lead-rubber apron that surrounded his lanky frame. As he strode about the reception area (while the screening room was cleaned and reset between cases), scarlet Perspex goggles sat attached to his face, keeping his sight adjusted to the limited light in which he had to work, colouring his eyes to an alien, blood-red glow. In addition huge, lead-rubber gauntlets swung each side of him, removing any concept of their contents, white gloved, human hands, all of which gave him an uncanny resemblance to a character from the previously popular, but scary, TV science fiction drama, "Quatermass." Nervous patients, awaiting their turn for his attention, looked on with alarm at this extraordinary presence prowling about; only his secretary was bold enough to interrupt his impatient promenade, but even she needed a very good reason for doing so.

The third radiologist, Dr Patterson was close to retirement and worked mainly at the smaller, cottage hospitals. He was a short tubby, bespectacled man with a quiet, gentlemanly manner and could do no wrong in Sister Aster's eyes. Rumours occasionally surfaced that in their prime this unlikely couple were indeed just that. I found it hard to imagine Sister Aster cuddling up to anybody but it explained her slightly warmer expression when he entered the department.

Two medical secretaries, ideally suited to their respective bosses, served these three consultants.

Doreen was a dark haired, rather demure lady, in her early thirties, who defended Dr. Weston-Smythe's private practice from all complainants. She had a great knowledge of medical terminology and often helped me out when I was befuddled, not only by a doctor's handwriting but what he was requesting. All the hospital's medical secretaries took shorthand and typed vast numbers of complicated words to the minute. I held them in great esteem.

Judy was the other secretary, who skilfully managed the moodiness of her boss Dr. Hugo.

She frequently exited his office smiling broadly at some jovial repartee between them but I never saw any other member of staff elicit humorous remarks from him. She was always bustling through the corridors of the department with sheaves of x-ray packages tucked under her arm on her way from a lengthy reporting session. Her lively personality complimented Doreen's demeanour and the two girls worked well together. They also shared the duties for Dr. Patterson.

Now, as promised Letitia; her official title, "Screening Technician," her unofficial, bawdy title, "Queen Bum of Room 1" because most afternoons she poked rubber catheters into at least two Barium Enema patients' anal orifices!

Letita, although unqualified, had been employed to assist the consultant radiologists in the screening room with their examinations of patients' alimentary systems, tasks all radiographers found tedious.

She was a very self-assured young lady of about nineteen, performing often unpleasant tasks with a showmanship of hauteur, defying anyone to deride her role. She had amazingly secured this position through family contacts, using the friendship of her retired father, an ex-army Colonel, with several consultants and members of the management committee, all of whom socialised within the upper echelons of Elmbridge. The Hospital Management Committee agreed unanimously to her employment in spite of Letitia being untrained and unqualified;

This all-powerful committee seemed happy to allow her to use dangerous x-rays without supervision. Clearly a case of "Who you know," not "What you know." To my surprise even Sister Aster found no fault in her appearance or behaviour, seemly overawed by the upper-class society contacts surrounding Letitia and her family.

Letitia's highly articulated vowels contrasted surprisingly with her appearance. She stood just less than five feet tall with dark curling hair pulled back into a fashionable "French pleat." However by always wearing black, court-heeled shoes her lack in height was significantly increased, this also helped to balance her, size 38 D cup, breasts, as they rose and fell under the lustful gaze of any male standing close by. Her lips glistened, stained scarlet (even at 8.30 in the morning) as she made the most of any opportunity to mix with promising young doctors, who sometimes visited the department to discuss case histories or "sit-in" on a screening examination. Her hunt was on for a marriage acceptable to Daddy! Letitia and the screening room deserve their own telling later.

Chapter 3

It was in Room 2, the general x-ray room, I first experienced the reality of the world; it shocked this naïve, protected teenager and brought home that there were evil people and events waiting, lurking for me to discover in the future.

Leslie and Marsa the two Junior Radiographers were sharing the GP, casualty and clinic workload one busy morning. Marsa was the newest junior of the two and was of Chinese decent. Her mixed parentage weighed heavily; ethnic diversity was rare outside London and she had grown up with an ever-expanding resentment of her heritage. She worked hard and skilfully but sadly I never spotted any signs of pleasure in her chosen career or outward compassion to extremely ill patients. On this morning it was break time and Marsa was having a well-earned cup of coffee when Leslie called to me for some assistance. Leslie was beautiful outside and in, loved by everyone. She gave me great encouragement, always defending me when Sister disciplined me in public. She was married to one of the hospital doctors, a senior registrar, who was much respected, so sometimes Sister would reprieve me purely to gain favour with Leslie.

As always Leslie was eager to include me in my chosen career by bringing me into contact with "hands-on" radiography; I, in turn, like a grateful puppy happily dropped my menial tasks to spend some valuable time with her. I rushed to Room 2, to follow a stretcher-trolley with Ray, a tall male nurse from casualty standing at the feet end, pushing it through the doorway of the x-ray room, while Leslie pulled it into the room from her end. Beside it, bent over the protective side rails, hung a slightly balding man, probably in his late thirties, his leather coat slung haphazardly over his shoulders. He was whispering and cooing into a small ear, framed with blonde curls, belonging to a young child of about 3-4 years.

She reached up and put her thin bony arms around his neck as he gently lifted her across onto the x-ray couch.

"Daddy, don't leave me, please!" she sobbed into his chest.

"No, precious, I will stay right here! I can, can't I?" he asked Leslie.

"You will need to wear a lead apron," she replied handing him a heavy, brown, lead-rubber garment, which he placed over his head causing his shoulders to sag with the weight.

Leslie turned to her small charge, "Tracey, when I take your pictures with my magic camera can you hold your breath like this?" she asked closing her mouth tightly and holding perfectly still to demonstrate.

"I think so," replied the child tremulously.

"Nothing is going to hurt you, we just shine our light where the picture will be," explained Leslie reassuringly.

"Don't worry princess, I will be here all the time my treasure," coaxed her father.

I fetched the film cassette and placed it in the film tray underneath her; Tracey was having a series of films to examine her ribcage and lung fields, then Leslie positioned the x-ray tube (camera) carefully over the little girl.

We walked quickly back to the protected area of the room for Leslie to make the exposures, as she called, "Hold your breath Tracey, keep really still please!" and to our surprise the little girl managed perfectly.

I changed the films over and called through the hatchway to the darkroom, "Stuart, please watch these films, child's chest & ribs."

"Ray, we'll leave her on the table until I've checked the films. Can you stay with her?" asked Leslie.

"Sure," he said sharply, "I ain't going no-where!"

Leslie and I went next door to the wet-viewing room to await the films. She put a finger to her lips to silence me, then, whispered, "Did you get a chance to read her form? Tracey didn't fall from a chair, she was punched."

I stood still, totally shocked and mouthed back, "child abuse?"

"Yes, and by the man fawning all over her now."

Stuart brought out the three technically perfect, developed films. I looked aghast as Leslie pointed out the breaks in the curvatures of three fractured ribs but fortunately there was no apparent lung damage.

I helped Ray push the child back to casualty watching her father caress her so tenderly. Surely Leslie was wrong he seemed such a loving dad.

We handed over Tracey to Sister's care and Ray walked back a way with me.

"Did she fall?" I asked him anxiously.

He turned to face me, angry and bitter, "Tracey's mum was in last week with a broken jaw; she said she fell in the garden! Her bruising fitted someone's fist; Tracey's bruising fitted someone's fist; that man is the only person living with them. That bugger of a father did that!" Ray's eyes were blazing.

"Haven't the p..p.. police been told?" I stammered close to tears, "My dad's in the police in London, I thought they protected children. Surely Tracey's dad should be arrested!"

Ray's voice was despondent as he told me, "The police came and his wife wouldn't say anything, 'cept she fell in the garden, the police said to us it's "a domestic," nothing we can do mate, he beats his wife that's her problem not ours," then Ray added, "The casualty doctor is ringing them now to report Child Abuse this time, but I bet he gets away with it. He's a charmer 'til he drinks, then watch out for your life!"

I couldn't let it go, "Why do they stay with him?" I persisted.

"Where they gonna go? They've no money, no family, no one will take them in and face his temper. What a mess; until domestics are called to count by the law there is no answer." Ray was calmer now but it seemed such a hopeless situation to both of us. In spite of everything little Tracey clung to her father as he carried her carefully out of casualty, softly kissing her cheek and comforting her. How long would it be before he lost his temper again, who would suffer mum or Tracey or both? It would be many years before the police forces got involved and refuge hostels housed and protected women and children. This was my first encounter with the shocking reality of domestic violence.

The third room specialised in kidney examinations, where two patients were examined simultaneously, separated by a rather wobbly lead-rubber screen. By doubling up in this way the waiting list for this procedure was kept down to about 6-8 weeks; kidney pain is excruciating, even that was far too long. These specific procedures took place most weekday mornings, often the radiographer in charge was one of the two seniors, Jeanette or Martin.

Jeanette, was a tall, elegant, married lady of about thirty, her husband was something important in the civil service and was frequently away from home. She was technically assured and surprisingly loyal to Martin, endlessly covering his regular disappearances for a "smoke" or visit to the ward of his girlfriend;

gossip about a romantic liaison between the two of them was always bubbling away in the background. I was in awe of her and although she was always kind to me especially in the episode with Mr. Grant, I never felt able to confide my many uncertainties to her.

Martin was a big, bluff, gregarious fellow in his early thirties with the ruddy complexion that displayed his love of hockey and the team's post-game, beery rewards or commiserations. Technically he was a little "slap-dash" but very speedy, a useful ability during a large fracture clinic when the corridor was overflowing with broken limbs encased in plaster attached to numerous patients. He thoroughly enjoyed his reputation as a womaniser having dated many of the nurses, all the way from first year students to ward sisters, one of which was his current flame. His jovial manner hid a more caring side, which I was to see in later tragic circumstances.

One Thursday morning two ladies were recumbent on x-ray couches, in Room 3, awaiting the presence of a junior doctor, who was coming to inject iodine based "dye" into their blood streams via a vein in their arms. This contrast fluid would then circulate rapidly around the body, quickly reaching the urinary system (kidneys and bladder), where it would show up these organs in detail on a series of x-ray films and how well the system was working. Using this procedure, blockages, tumours or non-functioning systems as well as many other diseases could be diagnosed. It was an extremely valuable investigation, important in setting patients towards the right treatment for their conditions and was known as an IVP (Intravenous pyelography). Jeanette carefully explained the process involved to both ladies and checked if they had any known allergies or if either of them suffered from asthma or hay-fever, which they both dismissed.

Suddenly, twenty minutes after he had been summoned, Dr. Meredith rushed into the room, his untidy mop of over-long hair falling over his eyes and his white coat flapping around him.

"So sorry I'm late couldn't get away from the ward round and you know what a "B" Old Kerrigan is, I'm sure he drew it out purposely knowing I had to be somewhere else. He hates other people *pinching his staff*!" All this was directed to Jeanette under his breath as he prepared the syringes for the injections, double-checking with her that the ampoule contents were correct.

"Hello Mrs. Penfold, can you please let me see your arm?" he asked as he rolled up the sleeve of her x-ray gown to reveal her cream, flabby extremity. Turning her arm palm upwards he tightened a tourniquet, just above the crease in her elbow and delicately felt around for a suitable vein. Her chubbiness made this exploration difficult but eventually he settled on the best one available.

"A small scratch coming, this might make you feel warm all over as it courses quickly around you, bit like a hot flush really," he joshed.

"Ooh nothing different then!" she giggled.

After the syringe of 40mls of "dye" had been injected he withdrew the needle and syringe and stepped into the protected area of the room so that Jeanette could take an immediate film, not wanting to miss the initial outlining of the kidneys, as the heart raced the contrast fluid round in the bloodstream.

Next it was Miss Harvey's turn. She was 60 years old, of slight, even scrawny build and looked up at Dr. Meredith rather apprehensively. She closed her eyes tightly as the tourniquet was applied but there was no problem finding an appropriate vein for her, as several bulged, blue and rope like through her white opalescent skin. With the needle safely in position the houseman glanced quickly at his watch, to see he should have been in attendance at Mr. Kerrigan's outpatient clinic ten minutes ago.

He increased his pressure on the plunger and forced the iodine based contrast into her blood stream as quickly as he could, withdrew the needle calling, "Ok Jeanette, have to dash, bye ladies!" then whisked through the door out of the department.

 Jeanette rushed back to take the immediate film calling, " Now Miss Harvey, breathe in please and hold your breath," but suddenly there was a raucous coughing fit coming from the patient, who struggled to sit up, vomiting foaming mucus over the side of the couch. Jeanette ran to her side grabbing a vomit bowl just in time to see Miss Harvey's eyes roll upwards and backwards as she fell unconscious back onto her pillow.

I happened to be in the wet-viewing room next door, hanging films to dry.

"Mary, quick Mary, run after Dr. Meredith and drag him back here, we have a severe reaction and collapse!" she commanded.

I fled up the corridor just in time to see the tail of his coat as he swept through the plastic flapping doors. "Doctor Meredith!" I shouted as I caught up with him and grabbed his arm, he turned indignantly, unused to being accosted in such a manner.

"Major IVP reaction! You have come to come back."

 To his credit he grasped the situation instantly and ran back down to the department, with me following at his heels as we rushed into Room 3.

Martin was drawing up a small syringe with adrenaline from the emergency tray and Jeanette was positioning an oxygen mask to cover Miss Harvey's nose and mouth.

In all this drama poor Mrs Penfold seemed to have been forgotten and was lying, shaking on her neighbouring couch.

Jeanette looked across, as she instructed me in a cool composed voice, "Take Mrs. Penhold to Marsa in Room 2 to continue her IVP."

I helped the shocked lady through the door, handing her over to Marsa's care, while Jeanette, Martin and Dr. Meredith propelled Miss Harvey, on a stretcher-trolley, speedily to casualty. Thank goodness a touch of pink had resurfaced on her previously, blue-tinged face as she was handed over to the expert care of Sister and the more experienced casualty doctor.

The two senior's having relinquished their charge, nipped through the outside doors to light up welcome cigarettes and take stock of their actions, knowing there would be an enquiry into this morning's drama.

Miss Harvey regained consciousness in casualty, but was transferred to the women's medical ward for observation and an overnight stay before being allowed home.

Sure enough, Dr. Aubrey Weston-Smythe conducted an enquiry that afternoon, as director and head of the department, to include all the staff involved that ill-fated morning. We dutifully filed into his office to be seated in a semi-circle around his desk, while Doreen sat to one side, her shorthand pad and pencil poised to record every word. It was a very formal and quite terrifying experience for me. Each of us relayed our part in the emergency, leaving Dr. Meredith to agree that he had been under pressure and had rushed off too quickly, but even so he seemed reluctant to accept that this had been a major factor.

Dr. Weston-Smythe looked up from Miss Harvey's notes and addressed all of us in severe tones, "In future, it will be department policy for all contrast media injections to follow these new instructions I am setting before you. Only 2mls of contrast are to be injected initially, followed by a 3-minute wait, to see if there are any adverse effects; then and only then can the remainder of the contrast be injected slowly into the patient. These instructions will be printed out and plainly displayed for all doctors to see in all the x-ray rooms. All radiographers will draw the attending medical officer's attention to this new ruling. Are there any questions?" he concluded, almost daring a riposte from the silent, subdued Dr. Meredith. He closed the enquiry saying, "We must consider ourselves and more importantly, Miss Harvey, fortunate that this episode did not result in a fatality." These strong, sober words had a great impact on me as I realised there were all sorts of dangers unknown to me hidden in x-ray examinations.

Chapter 4

The first point of contact for most patients, when referred for an x-ray examination was at reception; here they were served by Brenda the department's receptionist. She was an unpretentious local girl, who sat anchored to her desk from 9.00am-5.00pm excepting break and lunch times, when either Mrs. L., Stella and now me, as a nervous cadet nurse, relieved her taking this important seat opposite Room 1 and unfortunately Sister's office. Brenda was a very capable young lady, who recognised every GP scrawl and seemed to spend hours, holding onto one of the two department phones, trying to locate missing ambulance transport for attending and homeward bound patients. She was in early twenties, also looking for the perfect man, but with her rather plain features they didn't seem to come flocking around. It was rather a shame as she was a happy, spirited girl with a ready laugh, working under the eagle eye of Sister with amazing humour. She was generally attributed with being "the salt of the earth" a description I never quite understood but took to be complimentary.

Stella worked alongside Mrs. L. in their combined roles as Nursing Auxiliaries. She wore her cap perched on fluffy, smoke scented, peroxide blonde hair with permanently dark roots seeping through. Stella was always cheerful, full of gossip, though I never knew it to be malicious, she saw a joke in nearly everything and her ribald sense of humour helped to balance against the daily traumas that entered our lives. She worked hard, an unmarried spinster sharing and caring for an elderly friend in a small council flat. The department became her family; her job was her joy.

Ted fathered us all with great humour. He had retired early from the local police force and now enjoyed a far less taxing occupation. His role of department porter, lead him into every area of the hospital and through his kindness to all, x-ray had a pretty good reputation.

Connie was the filing clerk, a demanding but often boring role, which she performed without complaint. She bustled about filing and finding films throughout the day for the long, outpatient clinic lists. The lengthy, dry-film sorting bench situated between reception and the pokey, smoky staff tearoom, kept everyone busy. This sorting area was where all the films had their sharp corners cut off and rounded, names checked and side markers double-checked, so that no scandalous surgical error could be made by removing the wrong leg or kidney! Press reports of such disastrous cases put terror into the hearts of all those taking radiographs as X-rays can be viewed from both sides, making a location marker essential.

A senior member of radiographic staff checked every film taken, each day, for accuracy and severely disciplined any radiographer who made a mistake. The two medical secretaries then ceremoniously delivered the films to Consultant Radiologists for their expert interpretation, which was typed in a report and sent to the requesting physician.

Either side of the sorting bench stood row upon row of tall, sliding filing cabinets, packed in chronological order with large brown packets of x-ray films or yellow replacement cards hopefully telling where they had gone. The "lost x-ray" phenomena was common to every hospital in the land, to the extent that what ever the reason for a long wait at a clinic the excuse was invariably, "Sorry, we couldn't find your x-rays" often expounded unfairly. Connie was a spinster, living and caring for her elderly parents, who heroically gave her working life to filing packets of x-ray films and searching for those purported to be missing. Her straight dark hair was cut severely around her bespectacled face, where fine dark hairs sprouted above her upper lip and a few stray bristles emerged from her chin. Connie's steady, reliable manner kept us all sane, whilst clinic nurses flapped about her in a fluster, when their consultant demanded a set of films that had gone astray. She soaked up the dramas of the day with a soothing calm having heard it all before during her many years of service. Connie refused to panic even if "God" himself had demanded a set of irretrievable x-ray plates, missing presumed lost. Then one clinic day just that happened.

It was a busy surgical clinic morning, when suddenly Mr. Kerrigan, along with his entourage of Dr. Meredith, Clinic Nurse Baxter and cadet nurse Anna, swept into the department. Tucked into the lapel of his navy, pinstriped, suit sat a crimson rose bud, whilst a peaked white handkerchief edged out from his breast-pocket. Mr. Kerrigan was a tall, slim man of military bearing, his dark hair adhered to his head glistening with Brylcream and a neatly trimmed moustache perched over his upper lip.

"Ladies!" he commanded, "Your incompetence knows no bounds. My staff here has battled for days to recover the x-ray films of

Mrs. Spooner's chest and abdomen with sadly no success. I have had to come here in person to secure them, and I do not expect to leave your department empty handed!"

Connie set her mouth firmly, boldly squared her shoulders as she stepped up to face him, but before she could open her mouth in riposte Sister Aster's door was flung open.

Drawing her self up to her full height, her words lashed out at him, "How dare you speak to my staff in that tone! Leave my department immediately and do not return until you are able to apologise in full for your insufferable behaviour."

I don't believe anyone had spoken to Mr. Kerrigan like that since childhood. A deep purple flush crept from the tips of his ears through to the end of his thread-veined nose as he turned about and marched back to his clinic, accompanied by his astounded followers. Connie breathed her thank you to Sister Aster, who gave a rare chuckle and closed her office door quietly behind her. Brenda hurriedly searched the card file and discovered Mrs. Spooner had recently been discharged from Women's Surgical Ward. Ted headed off on a mission of pride to discover these films whereabouts.

Ten minutes later he reappeared clutching a well-worn package, "They had slipped down behind the nurses' laundry basket, probably had been left on top and then slid off when someone grabbed a fresh sheet, the ward's responsibility really but anyway Mrs. Spooner's films are found safely, honour restored."

He knocked on Sister Aster's door and with the precious find under her arm she clicked her heels to Mr. Kerrigan's clinic. She returned, head held high, clutching his crimson, rosebud buttonhole between her fingers, which she placed carefully in Connie's hand.

"I shall take it home and press it," announced Connie beaming delightedly, her reputation and the department's had been rightly restored.

An ever-open door lead from these filing cabinets through to the tiny staff rest room, wherein a wall cabinet, which contained white and green-ringed crockery hung above a white enamelled sink. A boiling kettle sat constantly hissing on a small, blue-flamed gas ring, next to an ashtray overflowing with dog-ends, while the top fan-light window was kept open in all weathers to extract rising columns of smoke. A door in the opposite wall of this cramped space lead to an inner sanctum, Dr. Hugo's office.

It was here that I had attended for interview and sat in awe of the great man, whose pale, equine face had been lit only from the three viewing boxes that faced him. His pallor reflected the nature of his work that mainly took place in darkened rooms; deprivation of natural daylight came with the job. He was an unpredictable man, charming and chatty on a good day, morose and irritable on a bad day. He loved cricket so that in the summer months a portable radio was permanently tuned into "Test match special," where the jovial tones of Brian Johnson livened up his office. The other two radiologists shared another office adjacent to the reception area. They both divided their hours between Elmbridge hospital and three other "cottage" hospitals (that were part of this Administrive Group) which had single x-ray rooms, so were never in the main department at the same time. The inevitable official meetings between all three doctors were held in the hospital boardroom, which gave enough space for their competing egos.

There was one last area that belonged to the x-ray department with which I had to familiarise myself. It was mysteriously known as "the woods." My shyness and ability to blush crimson had soon become renown, offering much temptation to tease me, which the ribald humour of the male nurses, porters and radiographers could not resist. Every day one of them would sidle up to me and whisper an invitation for a rendezvous,

"Come on Mary, I'll make your day really special, let's nip off to the woods. Just you and me!" Then winking knowingly, the teaser would disappear, chuckling at my discomfort.

In 1962 sexual harassment was an unknown offence and although there was never any malice in these asides, ribaldry such as this in today's "offence-free" working climate would be very risky. All I longed for was to join in with some smart response, instead my cheeks burned and I curled up inside, too naïve to act "cool," a phrase that was creeping in even then.

One quiet morning before the patients from fracture clinic had flooded down to x-ray the radiographers stood chatting around reception.

Connie was talking to Mrs. L. and I heard her say, "What a nuisance I've got to pop up to the woods for a set of old films, when I've a stack to sort out here for Mr. Tucker's orthopaedic clinic."

"Don't worry," said Mrs. L. "Mary's never been up there yet and its time to put all that teasing nonsense to bed, give me the key and I'll take her with me."

But Martin heard all this too and cut in, "No Mrs. L. I will take Mary and show her the ropes!"

I froze on the spot. "It's OK Martin, thank you but Mrs. L. will help me," I quickly chimed in as Connie handed him the key and to my horror a torch. He gave everyone a broad wink then steered me by the elbow up the corridor. So, leaving many chuckling voices behind us, we headed up the corridor towards the staircase leading to the "Private Ward," which was situated adjacent to "the woods". In the early sixties and for many years to come, Private Patients were greatly resented in NHS general hospitals. Most of the staff felt uncomfortable or even angry when *PP* was added to a patient's referral, for whatever requested examination, because they frequently overtook any waiting NHS patient for the same procedure. Hard-nosed consultants were seen fawning over these people and at Elmbridge the private ward was positioned in a very quiet area of the hospital next to the Doctor's residency. It was governed by the most severe sister, Sister Wilkins, who protected her charges from all basic staff members (other than those cleaning). The Private ward had its own lift, its doors opening alongside the door to "the woods." As we reached the top of the stairs there was no sign of activity, no sign of the fearsome Sister Wilkins but for once, I would have been delighted at her presence.

Martin unlocked the door and followed me in, alarmingly locking the door behind him. The lighting was so dim he needed to turn on the strong torch beam, revealing row upon row of filing cabinets full of x-ray films lurking in the gloom. Each cabinet represented a year. The two years prior to 1962 were kept downstairs with Connie but 1959 back to 1955 were housed here and our mission was to locate a set of films taken five years ago.

It took us nearly half an hour of poking and prodding fingers between tightly packed packages; there were hundreds of them, until I called out in relief, "I've got them they're here."

Perhaps all the lost hospital x-rays from around the country, I wondered, had surreptitiously found their way here.

As I tugged at the package I felt Martin's warm breath on the back of my neck and his hand slipping round my waist. I couldn't breathe, tension gripped every muscle and tendon as I poised myself, ready to kick, bite or punch him.

He turned me around to face him and burst out laughing, "Oh! Mary you poor little thing you look ready to kill me! I'm just winding you up, come on you would have been disappointed if I hadn't," he chortled, as if it was the world's best joke. "Here let me take the films," and he unlocked the door still chuckling all the way back to the department.

The others greeted us with cheers, I was mortified and with a burning red face fled to the loo to try and recover my composure. Of course, as I had gazed around, I realised why the woods had such a racy reputation, its hidden corners so dimly lit, were ideal for real life "doctor and nurses" games. No wonder the nudge wink brigade were enjoying winding me up. To my discomfort the "joke" had soon travelled along the "grapevine' leaving me to deal with endless tormenting of, "Who's a naughty girl locked up with Martin for half an hour, oooh!" and singing, whistling or humming, "If you go down to the woods today......"

Requirement for huge spaces such as the "woods" designated to x-ray to keep records for the obligatory six years, has ceased to exist, for the health world has become digital. Today storage facilities for hard copies of x-rays are redundant; instead patients' records are computerised.

To continue with the radiographic staff compilation, the next in line of seniority, amongst the radiographers, was Mr. Petrie, Deputy Superintendent. He was technically brilliant, understanding not only the workings of the human body and its anatomy but also the workings of all the heavy, awkward pieces of equipment housed in the department. He knew best how to manipulate the three key elements for successful radiographs, by bringing patient, x-ray tube and film together, to achieve incredible results even under the most difficult situations.

He was of an average height, slim build with a dry, mousey coloured, thatch of hair that never knew which way to lie and tufty eyebrows hovering over pale, hazel eyes; in short an unremarkable man. Sadly to match his lustreless appearance, he also lacked any personal skills finding social interaction very difficult, avoiding eye contact with others throughout a conversation, which made leading a team, giving explanations or reprimanding staff extremely awkward for all concerned. His reclusive nature prompted him to retreat behind closed doors with pen and paper, relishing sorting out some technical problem. During my cadetship he was an illusive person, disappearing like the wisps of smoke from his pipe, whenever I tried to ask his advice. Ironically it was his formidable knowledge that had secured the future for the prospective School of Radiography; making it a success would prove a mammoth task for such an introverted personality.

Finally, The Superintendent Radiographer, who was of course Sister Aster. Her accreditation of this position had developed many years previously, for at one time she had become involved with the rudimentary beginnings of diagnostic radiography and its expansion here at Elmbridge. In the late 1920's and early 1930's early x-ray exponents were selected from fully qualified nursing staff, who, left their bedside roles with the promise of entering into this unknown but exciting new field. Soon, as the realisation of how essential the whole concept of visualising the internal workings of the body had become, it became apparent that handling more elaborate equipment and acquiring photography skills would require a specialist staff, with specialised training beyond the nursing field. In 1932 the first "Schools of Radiography" appeared and although the "Society of Radiographer's was founded in 1920 their first professional conference came after the war in 1947. Sister Aster had then been away from her "hands-on" nursing career for too long having missed the experience needed for promotion to ward sister, she was neither, "Nurse" nor a newly-trained "Radiographer." There was no way back for her so in recognition of her pioneering x-ray work at Elmbridge, she was rewarded with the most senior position in the new x-ray department, however only in an administrative capacity. She became frustrated at having to oversee a staff, which had a greater expertise than she had accomplished, resentful of youngsters just starting out their careers, as they gained more knowledge than she had achieved, within two short years. No wonder her instinct was to make departmental life as difficult as possible for those such as me; knowing these skills was now beyond her reach. Sister Aster was neither nurse nor radiographer, she approached her imminent retirement unfulfilled and with rancour.

So it remained that just three senior radiographers, Mr. Petrie, Martin, Jeanette and the two juniors, Marsa and Leslie had to provide twenty-four hour care on every day throughout the year. In spite of the onerous task of working very long hours with possible sleepless nights, the "on-call" rota was popular.

Radiographers earned paltry pay, coming under a salary scale deemed "Professions Supplementary to Medicine" regulated by the Whitely Council, where it was still cited that enjoying a vocational occupation was more important than monetary reward, therefore making extra money from "out of hours" working brought not only a much needed bonus, but was financially, extremely necessary.

This x-ray department's hotchpotch of people formed a sizable x-ray staff within which I had to somehow fit. A single-sexed, Grammar School education had done nothing to prepare me for such a bevy of characters, each more than capable in their own field but all needing to work well together so that patients received the best possible service and also trying to maintain the well respected reputation of the x-ray department.

Except, just before I leave this issue, two of the most important ladies of our team didn't appear until five o'clock in the evening; the "cleaners," cheerfully referred to as Mags and Babs.

They kept "their department" spotless, no other cleaner was allowed to trespass; it was theirs and only theirs! Every surface was dust free, splashes of barium were washed away, flakes of plaster of Paris, wayward hairs all manner of medical debris were sucked from under x-ray tables and patient chairs to oblivion. Our department was "hospital clean" when that phrase meant the cleanest of clean, thanks to the devotion and hard work and pride of these two lovely ladies.

Chapter 5

The department had two portable machines. The first was a bulky, black monster that describing it as portable was a joke; only our porter or two male radiographers had a hope of coaxing it into movement. Then on a down slope (having been designed without brakes) it was almost impossible to stop. Its usage was to x-ray patients while they remained in their beds, either because they were badly injured in casualty, attached to hoists or electrical equipment that was not moveable or the severity of their illness made trundling them across the open courtyard from the wards, down the out-patient's corridor to the almost exiled x-ray department, too risky.

Another important role for the black machine was to enter the most hazardous and harassed setting for any radiographer, the operating theatres. Here operations came to a halt while a usually stressed, junior radiographer dived under the numerous sterile green operating sheets, which swathed the inert patient, trying to find some idea of what part of their anatomy she or he had located. Next, manoeuvre this awkward old x-ray machine to line it up with the all-important film underneath. Help was rarely given, so if any part of the sterile field became inadvertently contaminated during this burrowing, a sharp rebuke would quickly belittle the hapless practitioner. It was all very "hit and miss!"

Another complication arose around keeping the unconscious patient's body movements still. On a good day an obliging anaesthetist would control the patients breathing and halt it for the short exposure time required. Occasionally this request was refused so that the only solution to a clear picture was to judge the rise and fall of the patient's chest, press the exposure button and pray the timing was right. A successful outcome was accepted without comment by the attending doctors and nurses, however any failure would resound around the hospital gossip network quicker than the repeat could be taken. One poor junior radiographer produced her masterpiece to the gowned surgeon and his entourage whilst the film was still dripping wet from the developing tanks. She placed it on the viewing box with pride. Everything was as it should be. The position was right, the exposure correct however as the doctors crowded round to view the film, droplets of water met an exposed lighting wire from the viewing box and with a sharp bang all the theatre lights were fused. Of course the emergency circuiting cut in, allowing the operation to proceed but she fled in tears and was never allowed to forget this misdemeanour.

The second portable machine was known as "the suitcase portable." It did indeed, in its entirety, fit into a large metal box, vaguely resembling a suitcase but only a formidable weight-lifter could have carried it any distance, instead it was moved by wheelchair to the hospital transport car when an examination outside this hospital was needed.

The maternity hospital was situated about half a mile away. It had recently pioneered a "Special Care Baby Unit" (SCBU), where vulnerable newborns were hopefully to be steered towards survival. In those instances an x-ray picture of tiny lungs and beating heart gave the paediatrician valuable information. This was a job for the suitcase machine, itself requiring careful handling to protect the fragile filaments inside the x-ray tube head.

On a bitterly cold November afternoon, an urgent request was telephoned through to Brenda for a chest x-ray on a baby about three hours old. There was concern over the rapidity of his breathing rhythm and the degree of blueness around his lips. He had been born four weeks early and was in an incubator.

Leslie took control of the situation and because Marsa was at late lunch there was no one else to spare. "Mary can you give me a hand with a portable at the Mat. Home?" she asked. "If Sister says it's OK I'd love to come." I replied cheerily.

Permission was granted so I helped prepare the cassettes and lead aprons we needed, then we both huddled ourselves into outdoor coats while Deputy Head Porter; Jack brought the hospital car round. We set off chatting about how tiny this baby would be. At the Maternity Home, Jack lifted the heavy "suitcase" out from the car and carried it manfully into a rackety lift just beside the main entrance, which took us up to the SCBU.

Once safely delivered next to the incubator, it was up to Leslie and me to assemble it. I had never seen this equipment in use, but there was a sheet of instructions taped to the lid of the box, which we followed with total concentration in order to attach the right pole to the base. Next we fitted the trajectory arm into the pole, then with both our combined strengths we lifted the tube head onto this arm, screwed the clamp tightly and said muttered prayers that it wouldn't topple over. Finally an electrical socket had to be located, so I crawled on hands and knees under cots, chairs and behind cabinets to plug the wretched thing in! I wonder what today's health and safety officials would make of this awkward, spiteful equipment that nipped our fingers, broke our nails and wobbled precariously when moved.

We both put on lead rubber aprons and then covered those with white sterile gowns, making us look as large as Michelin Man in the tyre advertisements, facemasks finished off the ensemble. Leslie took our smallest cassette and we gingerly approached this tiny form.

Perched on his head was a blue knitted bonnet nearly covering his eyes. A soft muslin nappy, cut down in size still reached his ankles, where mini- blue bootees protected his feet.

His purple-tinged, finger-sized arms waved wildly, as if looking for an orchestra to conduct,

whilst both little hands clenched their fingers tightly into pink and white marbleised balls. A clear narrow tube was lightly taped to his cheek so that oxygen could be delivered through his nose without the risk of it being dislodged.

Baby Andrew Westgate, boy, weight

3lbs,

Height 19.5 inches born 12.05pm 25th November

1962

stated the blue-edged card, attached to his incubator, announcing the arrival of this new human being, who was already struggling to survive.

Leslie placed the cassette inside a small pillowcase and then ever so gently she lifted him up, while I slid the hard film under his upper body. An anxious nurse looked on monitoring his reaction to such treatment. Leslie quickly positioned the x-ray tube over him, placing a tiny piece of lead rubber over his genitals to protect them from the scattered rays. He may want to become a father himself one day so no radiation was going near whatever sperm he may have tucked away. There was no way he could hold his breath or Leslie time his breathing accurately, she just made the exposure and then gingerly slid out the film. We slipped off our gowns and aprons and ran out to Jack waiting in the car and rushed back to our x-ray department.

"SCBU baby's chest film. Stuart, please watch really carefully!'
Leslie shouted through the darkroom hatch and sure enough only
minutes later he brought out the freshly developed, dripping wet
film to us, anxiously waiting, in the viewing room.

"Oh my goodness! Do you see the huge size of his heart against
those tiny lungs; not much air in either of them. Oh dear, doesn't
look good!" Leslie wailed, anxiously studying the black and white
image. "I'll take the film to Dr. W-S for a quick report, then you
can dash it back with Jack. I'll have to stay in the department as its
getting really busy."

X-ray Report Baby Andrew Westgate   Date 25-11-62

*This portable chest x-ray shows a considerably enlarged heart
with immature, partially air-filled, lung fields typical of congenital
heart disease. Possible diagnosis co-arctation of the aorta."*

Dr. A. Weston-Smythe Consultant Radiologist

Later Leslie translated the report for me, possibly Baby Andrew's
main blood vessel leading from the heart, called the aorta, was
almost blocked for some reason, malformed and narrowed during
the early stages of pregnancy; therefore his blood supply could not
be properly pumped around his body, this made the heart engorged

and swollen, causing heart failure and if untreated death. Baby Andrew needed an operation to widen this main blood vessel very quickly, but as he was so tiny and this was specialised surgery his chances weren't good. Sadly, we learnt he never became well enough to transfer to the cardiology unit, at the Great Ormond Street Children's Hospital and later that week he died.

The suitcase portable was also quite frequently called into use in one other small hospital on the outskirts of Elmbridge, where an amazing lady, Ellen spent her life. This was the isolation hospital housing long-stay tuberculosis patients. This dreadful disease was still present in 1962 although thank goodness vaccination was beginning to control its spread. However in this instance it was not a patient who had contracted TB, but a patient who had contracted polio at the age of nineteen with devastating consequences.

Ellen was in need of a portable chest x-ray. She was now thirty-eight years old, her life support maintained solely by placing her body, from the neck down, within a huge metallic casing known as an "Iron-Lung," leaving only her head visible, framed angelically by soft fair curls. It allowed her immobile life to continue but deprived of fresh air, wind, rain or sunshine this absence of weathering left her complexion free from ageing. Her skin was, clear of wrinkles, smooth and pale, except for her lips, which glistened with a pretty pink lipstick.

All her muscles had been affected by the paralysis of polio so that she was unable to breathe without the continual backward and forward rocking of this coffin like contraption. The rocking motion dragged her diaphragm down, sucking air into her lungs then as the tilt was reversed so the diaphragm pushed the air out of them again. As well as the essential breathing the "lung" allowed her to speak in whispered gasps. Unfortunately to add to her predicament she was very vulnerable to chest infections, each episode required a chest x-ray to determine how severely her lungs were infected. Whenever these circumstances arose, two radiographers armed with the suitcase portable were taken by hospital car to the isolation hospital where they set up the equipment next to the iron-lung. The difficulty was that movement and any static photography do not go well together. In order to get a diagnostic x-ray the iron-lung had to be stilled while the exposure was made. This was an anxious procedure for both Ellen and the radiographers, who for once had no need to ask the patient to hold her breath because Ellen was unable to breathe until, with gasps of relief, the "lung" rocked again. The only time Ellen became distressed was when a storm could be heard rumbling in the distance knowing she had to rely on the efficiency of the portable generator, which stood close by to take over whenever a power cut occurred.

Over these incarcerated years she had become a watercolour artist, using her mouth to hold the brush and paint so skilfully, so delicately, with such fine brushwork, that many of her pictures decorated our walls in yearly calendars and Christmas cards. Ellen became one of the most famous of the "Foot and Mouth"artists as they were known. This inspiring lady achieved a quality of life, which astounded all the staff and visitors that came to know her; she lived into her middle fifties.

My working week included Saturday mornings from 9.00am-12.30pm when only a minimal staff was present. This particular Saturday morning, Stella, Stuart and I were supporting Jeanette, who was the "on-call" radiographer for the whole weekend, day and night. About 12.05pm she popped her around the hatchway of the reception desk, where I was seated, sorting filing cards, "Mary are you in a hurry to get away today?" she asked.

"No, I don't have anything much planned, just some shopping in town so my Aunt's not expecting me back 'til later. Why?"

"Well I've just heard that a bad RTA (road traffic accident) is on its way, two carloads of injuries. Stuart is going to stay on in the darkroom, I wondered if you could be a runner for me as they're bound to want some portable films?"

"Sure," I replied, then stopping to listen we quickly picked up the sounds of ambulance sirens getting louder and closer until their wailing cries stood outside the casualty entrance.

Suddenly Jeanette's pager started its urgent bleeping, "Right off we go. Mary, stack up different sized cassettes while I put on a 'lead' apron. Here's Jack now. Can you get the portable up to casualty?" she asked him.

Without needing to reply he grabbed the big black machine's handle and pushed this heavy, awkward piece of equipment as fast as he could up the sloping corridor; rushing passed, we arrived before him.

It was mayhem in the small casualty department as the less urgent patients were dispatched back to the waiting room, (it would be some hours now before they would receive attention) whilst ambulance men and policemen struggled in with stretcher cases and the walking wounded. The most severely injured, a young man, Robert Brown, aged 18 years, was quickly assessed by the casualty officer, Dr. Khan, who directed him to be put straight onto a specialised x-ray trolley, suitable for portable films to be taken.

"Over here!" I heard the doctor call out to Jeanette, "I need a skull series and chest x-ray on this young man as quick as you can," Jeanette pushed her way through, clearing a path for Jack to position her machine alongside the trolley. I followed and handed Jeanette the largest film for the chest x-ray. I was so overwhelmed by the dramas around me that I had hardly glanced at the young man recumbent before me, then my senses clicked in, first my nose, next my eyes registered his appalling injuries.

Blood has a very distinctive smell. There was a lot!

To my horror it looked as if his face had been sliced in two. A huge, gaping furrow of mangled nasal and cheekbones divided his features in a bloody, gungey mess, but even more horrific his left eyeball was hanging from its socket; worse still he was conscious! Nothing in life had prepared me for a sight such as this. I held my breath.

"You cannot be sick, you cannot faint!" I ordered myself as Jeanette prepared to take Robert's chest x-ray.

"Hold your breath!" she commanded and amazingly he obeyed. She passed me the film then continued, "I am going to gently lift your head and replace the pillow with a foam pad which won't show on the x-ray plate."

She turned to me again so that I could hand it to her, but at that moment I caught sight of his eye, although still attached, rolling outside its socket and froze. "Mary now, please!" she ordered. Quickly, brought to my senses, we exchanged the pad for the blood soaked pillow, which I thrust into Sister's hand, turned tail and fled. Clutching the chest film cassette I dashed back to the darkroom. Stuart grabbed the cassette and whipped the darkroom door closed behind him.

Outside I stood shaking, panicking. What to do? Should I wait? Go back? Take more cassettes? I was still terrified that I would do the unforgiveable and pass-out. Oh! This was all too awful, how was I going to cope?

Suddenly the darkroom door opened and Stuart pushed the dripping film into my hand.

"Here take this," Stuart said firmly, "You're shaking Mary. Go on now, you'll be fine. Just don't drop it," he said; his calm, measured tone steadying me as I grabbed the precious chest x-ray and charged backup the corridor to casualty.

Jeanette had completed two skull films so I quickly returned to have those developed in the darkroom, leaving Dr. Khan studying Robert's chest film against a brightly lit viewing box. After two more trips a full set of chest, skull and facial bone x-rays were complete, to reveal three fractured ribs with some lung damage, a fractured frontal skull bone and smashed nasal and cheekbones.

What a mess!

Dr. Khan quickly explained, "Robert's skull and facial injuries have resulted from a high-speed impact with the windscreen sun-visor, which has cut through his flesh like butter, along with rib fractures from compression against the steering wheel."

The emergency team did a wonderful job in the initial repair of Robert's horrific facial injuries, which were to be even further improved over time by plastic surgeons in a specialist unit.

Six months later Robert returned to our x-ray department for a follow-up series of films. His facial scarring tracked from his forehead, down the left side of his nose to his upper lip, like a thin pink ribbon; over the years it would fade even more. Wonderfully, his eye had been safely replaced in its socket; miraculously the optic nerve had remained intact so that his vision in this left eye had made enough progress for him to return to work, as an apprentice carpenter. Thankfully Robert's future looked good.

Of course, eventually, Ernest Marples, Government Transport Minister, enforced the wearing of seat belts for all motor vehicles' drivers and front-seat passengers. At first this law was extremely unpopular, but proved to be the saviour of many lives and reduced the numbers of series injuries, however it was still many years before back seat passengers were also to be included.

It had been a shocking introduction to casualty work for me, but strangely enough this became the type of radiography I grew to love best.

Chapter 6

It was late November; a persistent fog masked the countryside with a rawness that penetrated the thickest coat. My parents had moved to their new home, on the outskirts of Elmbridge, leaving James to share a flat in Battersea with his old schoolmate. Thank goodness he had made a wonderful recovery from his encephalitis and had returned to work. Mum, of course, worried endlessly about him but I had returned to the nest, a new nest ready to be created with her in-born, warmth and love. Dad had started his new position with local government as an education welfare officer and was enjoying the regular hours, with the added bonus of work-free weekends. Mum was thrilled to be back in her home town, surrounded by her six brothers and two sisters with all their families. The siblings were very supportive of one another, but as the youngest of the nine she had to be prepared to face the inevitable fact that she would probably out live them all.

As the weeks progressed my duties expanded. Sister decreed I should work in the wet-viewing room to improve my loading and unloading of the drying cabinet. A pretty simple occupation you would think however it was primed with all sorts of pitfalls for me to encounter. Each shiny, wet plate was suspended in a wire frame throughout the developing, fixing and washing process, until after thirty minutes in the final wash it could be dried. The emulsion of the wet sheet of film was very vulnerable to damage at this stage and required careful handling. It had to be gently slid out from its supporting hanger and clipped with pincers to a metal bar, which then hung in the drying cabinet like a coat in a wardrobe. These plates varied in size from large films for chest, abdomen and pelvic x-rays, to small sheets bearing images of fingers, toes, wrist bones, nasal bones or other smaller body parts. It made sense then to hang the larger sheets on the bottom rack with the smaller ones above.

The perils that awaited this "simple" task were already lining up for me. Transferring the film from frame to hanger inadvertently produced the occasional scratch to the emulsion, which might hamper the correct diagnosis being read from the image.

The hot breeze circulating the drying cabinet sometimes caused two wet films, that were positioned too close together to meet, embrace and stick in such a tight clasp that they dried welded to each other; so that not just one image was defaced but two.

The consultant radiologists demanded their screening films took priority drying space, in order that they could report on the day's session, have the reports typed and signed before they left the department. Causing two or more of their films to stick, be scratched or damaged in any way was considered a serious crime as no patient wished a repeat barium procedure, also additionally, unnecessary radiation was now known to be detrimental to the human body; it was essential to keep x-ray dosages minimal.

The result of any undiagnostic film was a recall of the patient for a repeat examination. Radiographers dreaded the "recalled patient," who would be terrified that some appalling anomaly had been discovered in their anatomy. Even the most affable of the radiographic staff became very angry, if the cause for the repeat had occurred in the processing system, knowing that the patient's confidence in their radiographic ability had been damaged.

During these days I had daily contact with the casualty and clinic nurses as they came to take instant wet films to show their respective doctors, then returning them to me for drying.

My cousin Daphne was a third year student nurse, at Elmbridge, in the same set as Ray, who was still currently working in casualty, so he and I got along really well. She was four years older than me, not so tall but her slight build, fair hair and glasses gave us a noticeable physical resemblance; in fact we were often taken as sisters. She had an eventful social life involving the mixed bag of male and female nursing students who formed her set. They all relished the increasing freedom young people were now experiencing as the more liberal attitudes spread rapidly throughout the country, freeing previously held inhibitions, especially between the sexes.

Daphne was an excellent nurse, now nearly qualified she was alert and ready to deal with any emergency. One evening, while dining with her current boyfriend in a local restaurant, a man seated at the next table started to cough and choke, his complexion turning beetroot red.

She leapt from her chair, and in one incredible movement, heaved him upright away from his table; then grabbed him around his abdomen, thrusting upwards under his diaphragm with such force that a lump of steak was ejected from his mouth. "Now breathe, deep breath, come on!" she commanded as he gurgled and gagged; then all at once a huge intake of air, filled his lungs and his purple face began to lighten. He sagged to his seat, where his wife enveloped him in her arms, tears streaming down her face. Daphne had quietly returned to her place as the couple finally realised she had saved his life. The wife came over and hugged her tightly, then turned to the waiter and ordered a bottle of champagne to be brought to Daphne and her boyfriend's table. An evening neither party would ever forget.

One morning, while Ray waited for a set of films, he asked teasingly, "Mary do you miss the bright lights and the high life in London?"

"Yes of course I do!" I answered taking the bait, "I miss dancing at Streatham Locarno and Wimbledon Palais, I miss ice skating, I miss the choice of cinemas, three within twenty minute of where I lived and I miss swimming. There were two pools nearby! What's to do here?" I replied heatedly, boasting about all that I had given up to live in Elmbridge.

"Ok," he grinned "steady on! I can see you meant that didn't you? Can't match the ice-skating that's for sure, still maybe we can rectify the swimming, as the army lets nurses and ambulance men use their pool, at the Garrison, on a Thursday evening every week.

Daphne comes so I'm sure it would be OK for you to come too."

I felt the flush colour my cheeks, ashamed at showing off to Ray, only to be repaid with kindness. 'Oh thank you I should love that. It's Thursday tomorrow do you think I can come?"

"I'll check with Daphne and let you know," he replied, spraying droplets of water everywhere, as he swung a handful of wet films around and walked out into the corridor.

Elmbridge had been a garrison town to many, many regiments traced back historically to Queen Boudicca so its sports facilities were superb. An athletics track was loaned out to various clubs, horsey people could utilise the jumping arena and the swimming pool was available, to selected clubs, for use in the evenings. It's hard to image in today's, fearsome, terrorist climate such an open exchange of army land and property but I'm afraid we took it for granted, even seeing it as a public right. However on this occasion no other members of the public could use the pool as Thursday's pre-booked evening was allocated solely for hospital and ambulance staff.

I was delighted to be included to be invited to a social event, so that evening I cycled off eagerly with my swimwear and towel stuffed in my saddlebag, anticipating a pleasant hour of fun and swimming. I was sixteen years old; the youngest by far in this group of late teen and early twenties nurses, joining ambulance men aged between nineteen and forty.

Oh boy was I naive!!

This was after all the early 60's with its new premise of "anything goes;" the evening to come was certainly going to live up to that! As I stood, alone, on the edge of the pool, shivering slightly from a growing feeling of unease, I began to realise that the sole aim of the water sport, splashing before me, was to "de-frock" or more appropriately de-costume any member of the opposite sex in a riotous grabbing session, groping whichever part of their anatomy could be exposed. Cautiously I lowered myself into this frenzy and once in the water I found out very quickly that there were no rules, no etiquette, no hope of declining these exuberant activities, survival became my only pursuit. I clung to the side of the pool in horror only to be jumped on from above and pulled under the surface.

I enjoyed swimming but was not a particularly strong swimmer so my reaction to being forcibly submerged was one of sheer panic. I gasped for air, struggling to the surface with arms flailing and horrified yells, to fight off my attacker's attempts to tug off my costume! Blindly, without glasses I had no idea where my cousin was and in all truthfulness I feel sure she was too involved in all the grappling and groping to have cared. I wriggled and squirmed until my attacker went off in search of more willing prey, of which there were many. I splashed and belly-flopped my way to the steps, slipping and climbing out whilst my backside was walloped hard with great delight by a huge, hairy-chested, moustached, monster. I fled back to the changing rooms, pulled my clothes over my wet costume and tore out to un-lock my bicycle, pedalling as hard as if the devil himself was behind me, to the safety of home. I charged upstairs, stripped off clothes and swimsuit, and then, although still somewhat damp, wrapped myself into the comfort of my pyjamas and dived into bed. No way was I going to describe the evening's horrible experience to my mother knowing she would have "grounded me" forever.

It seemed I was far too chaste; nowhere near ready for the permissive society heralded by the sixties.

Thankfully, I was spared the embarrassment of seeing Ray the next day, as when I arrived Friday morning, Sister decided I was ready for a change and sent me off to help Stella in the sluice room.

In 1962 some sterilisation of equipment took place in the department, for there were no disposable items. The department held only two sets of barium enema equipment (the maximum number of cases each session), which meant the cleaning and sterilising of barium enema equipment, ready for re-use, was a very important part of Stella's day. It consisted of long lengths of rubber tubing, rubber ball-shaped valves and rubber inflatable catheters. This network of piping was suspended from large glass cylinders (containing liquid barium), linked together for the administration of the warmed fluid into a patient's anus or "up the bum," as Stella colloquially described this examination. The undignified route taken by the barium enema process, required the deflated, balloon end of the catheter to be greased (not too much else it would slip out!) then pushed into the exposed anal orifice. This was all very uncomfortable and embarrassing; at least it was to me, let alone the patient! The purpose of the ball-valve, which pumped air into the balloon collar around the catheter, was to help the patient keep the tube in their rectum, in the hope that the warmed contents now flowing through into the bowel would stay put!. Occasionally the patient's desire to empty became too much and with a voluble explosion….. catheter, air and fluid were expelled with great force, spattering anyone or anything within range.

At the end of the procedure (if all had gone to plan), the large volume of barium fluid introduced into the bowel was siphoned out, gravitationally, through the tubing by placing the glass cylinder on the floor below the patient's body level. Then to the relief of all, the catheter was removed from the patient, who left the room at great speed for the nearest loo to evacuate any remaining barium. Any patients waiting in turn for the same examination watched, with unbearable anxiety, the hurriedly departing figure, leaking a few white drips and drops on to the floor as he or she rushed passed.

The cleaning and sterilising of this conglomeration, after use, was acknowledged to be quite an unpleasant but necessary task that took place in the adjoining sluice room. At the end of each session, with her customary good humour, Stella pulled on thick yellow rubber gloves and armed with a large, stiff nylon brush scrubbed the barium and other unsavoury deposits from the glass cylinders. Carefully she wrapped the washed cylinders in a muslin cloth and immersed them in a large tank of boiling water to bubble away for twenty minutes. All the

Rubber tubing, valves and catheters had to be dealt with in a similar manner before drying and reassembling for usage the following day.

Stella became my new tutor, as I made my progression from "wet-viewing" room to sluice, where I had to learn quickly to overcome (or at least disguise) any reluctance in dealing with bodily fluids and odours. There would be no consideration made to any staff member who shied from such drudgery; I knew I just had to get on with it. Fortunately Stella's unflappable good humour made the most unpleasant task tolerable as we jostled and joked in the sluice's confined space, window wide open whatever the weather.

Once cleaning all the equipment had been completed we turned our attention to the consultant radiologist's white, cottoned gloves, which he wore under the huge, heavy lead-rubber gauntlets. These were worn to ease the friction and pressure of the necessary hand protection. Stella washed then bleached them to white perfection. At the end of the day the dry, gleaming glass cylinders were hung, back on their supporting drip stands, their attached tubing and catheters now squeaky clean.

Again, the cleanliness issues of today's hospital departments never existed whilst nursing auxillaries like Stella took such a pride in their role, earning the respect of everyone, even the perfectionist Sister Aster.

As I walked out of the sluice room, after a third day of rendering dirty enema equipment spotless, Sister summoned me to her office.

"Cadet Nurse, tomorrow I want you here by 8.30 a.m. You must be prompt as you are to assist Letitia in preparing the screening room ready for the morning session. There are six patients booked. You will get them changed and then learn how to set up the trolley. If and I mean *if* you deal with this competently and *if,* Dr. Hugo is in agreement you will remain with Letitia and attend the screening session. You will watch, not touch anything. Is that clear!! Wait here while I discuss this with Dr. Hugo."

Having delivered the longest dialogue ever to me she hurried off to his inner sanctum as I finally managed to breathe out in a whisper, "Yes of course I'll wait. Thank you Sister."

A few moments later she emerged from his office, "Be here tomorrow at 8.30 in the morning, not a minute later," she ordered, bringing a huge smile to light up my face.

I must have passed some sort of test; perhaps dealing with the rather smelly, dirty enema equipment without fuss had gained me favour. Whatever the reason I was delighted; at last I was to have proper, first-hand contact with patients.

Chapter 7

Somehow I need you to step inside that long gone world of fluorescent radiography!

Step into the room with me. Look how the room's windows are obscured by black heavy war-like roller blinds. See the huge, black-insulated, cable loops, hanging grotesquely from the ceiling like ominous nooses waiting to claim their victim. Some lead to the control desk, some to the boxed, oil- submerged valves and some to the x-ray tube beneath the couch. A large removable step is being attached to the bottom edge of the couch; next, the whole apparatus is driven into an upright position by a motored control.

X-rays will beam through the couch surface, through your body until they hit the fluorescent screen causing shadows of bone and barium. The lights are off, it is pitch black, and then, a torch-light beam shows you how to take up your position on the step of the upright couch with your back flat against it. Next the screening carriage presses closely on to your chest as it moves all over your body (it has an added compression plate, to squash into your flabby tummy).

Shapes come and go as your eyes become more used to the darkened room. You clutch the sole handle provided with a wet palm as a voice commands you to drink thick, sticky gunge from a small glass.

"Hold it in your mouth, don't swallow until I tell you!" comes the command.

It tastes of chalk and clings, doggedly to your teeth.

"Swallow!" and you try, really try, gagging, at last some globules relent as they follow gravity, travelling downwards from your throat.

"Don't move, hold your breath!"

The force of the voice makes you jump; then you stand rigid, not daring to disobey. At last further globules follow down, you breathe with relief, "done it," you silently applaud yourself and wait to be helped down from that cage, but instead a larger beaker is thrust into your out stretched hand in exchange for the little glass.

The first was the hors d'oevres; the second is the main course.

As instructed you drink and swallow then retch but barium is too heavy to be "sicked up," so like it or not you now have a belly full with an intrusive heavy gloved hand pushing and pressing all around your gut.

Now, suddenly you are on the move. The couch is being pulled, backward and downward, a hastily grabbed pillow is being pushed under your head as your whole, barely lit world goes upside down. Your head is now thirty degrees lower than your feet. Disembodied hands clasp around your ankles and you cling fast to the handle as the pillow begins to slip away.

 You clutch at pillow with your free hand then,

"Hold your breath!" shouts the voice, but you can't even catch it in your inverted state.

Suddenly, just as quickly, without warning, you are brought level again. The clashing & banging of spot film taking has stopped, the heavy gloved hand that pressed into your gut has gone, along with its phantom command voice; this time it is over!

The clamming screen carriage swings away from your body, as you are gently pulled upright and allowed to sit dizzily for a few moments. Released at last outside, re-united with your belongings, you look around, nothing outside has changed, other people await their turn but thank god you are back safely. Your turn is over. In these days before adrenaline packed, theme park rides existed, this experience came as close as any!

(Many Shoe Shops at this time proudly offered mini versions of this screening technology. With a foot inserted into the fitting machine an x-ray of a customer's foot structure showed the bones fitting snugly into a pair of shoes, glowing green with radiation. This quirky innovation was hastily withdrawn, when the danger of pointing x-rays upwards at an unsuspecting purchaser's genitals was revealed!)

I arrived early at 8.15 am and grabbed a cuppa with Mrs. L.

"You look perky this morning," she smiled, "looking forward to the screening room antics are you?"

"Yes I can't wait but I have to be so careful not to do anything wrong, I'm excited but a bit nervous too" I replied.

Just at that moment Letitia made her grand entrance into the tearoom. Her spotless, white coat covered an ample, lifted bosom and her scarlet painted lips impatiently summoned me to obedience. "Come along," she ordered. "Hurry up! I need you to get the patients changed immediately they arrive." She handed me a pile of freshly laundered white gowns and a second heavier pile of striped dressing gowns.

"Men strip down to their vests and pants and keep shoes and socks on, women take everything off except their knickers and shoes, " she instructed. "Bra straps with their metal fastening may obscure something important on the films," she volunteered, then spun around hurriedly towards her prestigious domain to prepare the room for the morning's work.

 Footsteps approached down the out-patient corridor and stopped at our reception desk. I hurried over to find a small, wiry man with a clipped, grey moustache, dressed smartly in a blue blazer, neatly creased trousers, white shirt, sporting a blue and red striped tie.

He cleared his throat, "Major Blythe for barium meal this morning at 9.00 am," he announced with authority, I almost felt him stand to attention while I entered his details into the register.

"Right sir I will show you the way to the changing rooms," I declared confidently as I lead him round to the row of small empty closets. I repeated the changing instructions Letitia had given to me; then added, "Mr. Blythe…"

"Major!" he interrupted sharply.

"Sorry *Major* Blythe, when you are ready, return to the reception area where there is seating outside the x-ray room, please bring all your belongings with you."

I walked away quietly smiling, that once he was clad in a hospital gown, with knobbly knees and thin veined legs exposed to the world, any title was pointless. One thing I had learned already, which helped me cope with pretentious people of any sort; once we are stripped down to the flesh, we are all are the same.

By 8.45 am all six patients were seated in total silence on the bench opposite the reception desk, outside Room 1. A young, still spotty youth studied his watch with intent, another more robust figure gazed into his surroundings seemingly without interest, a small middle-aged lady sat clicking her knitting needles at great speed, whilst the other three peered at the floor or examined their hands in finest detail. All six fruitlessly tried to cover their exposed knees with the shrunken, white hospital gowns while gathering their battered dressing gowns tightly around as far as they would reach.

Suddenly they all looked up expectantly as the tall, imposing figure of Dr. Hugo swept into the department. He carried a copy of the Times newspaper under his arm, his long trench-coat billowing out behind him.

He nodded a general "Good morning!" and disappeared into his office. Five minutes passed until he emerged with a huge, single-sided, brown, lead-rubber apron draped around his lanky frame. His eyes were concealed behind the bulbous red goggles (which helped his vision adapt to the minimum light available in the screening room). He carried oversized gauntlets in his white gloved hands, while he strode around the reception area as if looking for a spitfire to fly.

Letitia had previously drawn the blackout blinds at each window and positioned the foot-rest at the bottom of the now upright x-ray table. On a nearby trolley stood six small shot glasses, in a row, each containing the white thickness of undiluted barium. Behind these were six plastic beakers, three quarters full of a diluted mixture of barium and water.

There were several sizes of film cassettes ready for spot pictures to be taken, tucked behind the lead-glass, protected control desk, whose mysterious meters had been set to read the correct amperage and voltage. The clashing of these forces of power against a tungsten target caused x-rays to flow from the x-ray tube beneath the table top, on their directed path, penetrating the patient's body, until they finally bombarded the moveable fluorescent screen, where the negative image glowed eerily in the blacked out room.

The barium meal session was about to begin.

I pulled a heavy, double-sided, green protective apron over my head and felt my shoulders sink under its weight.

Letitia, who wore hers with panache, switched on an "usherette's" torch as she summoned; "Major Blythe, come in please." She steered him by the elbow, whilst directing the torch beam towards the slightly raised foot rest. "Step up with your back turned against the platform behind you. Give me your hand so that I can show you where you can find the handle."

He swapped over his tightly clenched handkerchief into his other hand (most patients carried the long-forgotten aid of a comfort cloth, in the form of a hanky) and grabbed the located handle with relief.

"Turn half-way to your left and take this small glass into your left hand," came the booming, disembodied voice of Dr. Hugo as Letitia placed the vessel into Major Blythe's shaking hand.

I took up my permitted position directly behind Dr. Hugo as my eyes slowly adjusted to the darkened room. Gradually I focused on the, green tinged, glowing screen and film carriage, which the radiologist manoeuvred adroitly, tracking Major Blythe's body, from the top of his head slowly sweeping down to his hips. The Major had become a digestive-system atlas, as one unpalatable mouthful of concentrated barium paste slowly slid (by gravity alone) down his gullet into his stomach. This was no culinary delight!

A black ribbon image unfurled on the screen, as Major Blythe's oesophagus slowly filled with thick barium, outlining the full-length of his guttural tubing.

Dr. Hugo ordered, "Don't move. Hold your breath!"

Major Blythe stood to attention, responding by instinct to a superior's command, whilst the banging and crashing of a large x-ray film cassette was propelled across his chest for three spot films to be taken. The film carriage moved back and Letitia dived into position quickly exchanging the exposed cassette for a fresh, different sized one and hurried back to place those first film-shots behind the protective screen. She twisted and turned control knobs altering the exposures for the next images. I watched her speed and anticipation as the procedure continued, with grudging respect. Unqualified she might be but she certainly knew her job.

To be any use at all in this environment I had to master exchanging film cassettes after the exposures had made. This action harboured yet another peril. The cassettes or thin metal boxes, only allowed x-rays to pass through one side to record the image on the inner film; the other side was lead lined to stop x-rays burning right through to the operator. To place a cassette in the carriage the wrong way round rendered the film blank.

 This was the greatest sin imaginable!

After Major Blythe's examination had finished, one by one all remaining five patients were put through the same procedure. At the end of the session Letitia and I carried large metal film carriers containing many dripping wet radiographs, from the wet room through to Dr. Hugo's office. We held each negative in front of him as he checked each patient's images. Satisfied he had successfully recorded all the relevant information for each case, he turned with a rare smile and said, "Well done girls they can all go home, eat and drink normally." We were dismissed.

Later that week I was given the role of film changer. I practised changing film cassettes for several hours in daylight. Speed was of the essence so that barium shadows still occupied the bit of gut that was deemed important. Barium went one way, down, leaving only one chance to get it right. No one wanted to repeat the procedure for something missed, most of all the gunged up patient! All went well for the first two patients and as my tense movements slowly loosened the task became easier; then disaster struck!

I had quickly loaded the long serial cassette, which took four shots of the duodenum and its duodenal cap, where benign and malignant ulcers often hid. But as I reached to remove it at the end of the four exposures my heart stopped; nothing would be recorded on it, it was back to front!

Sometimes the frozen silence of horror, from a consultant discovering a minion's blunder, was more devastating than any raging chastisement.

"*Another* serial film please!" came the icy instruction, as mortified, I forced a second long cassette into the waiting jaws of the carriage.

I stood shaking, appalled that the poor patient had now to imbibe even more barium sulphate and receive a greater dose of radiation because of my carelessness.

Letitia quickly took over for the remainder of the session as I retreated in shame behind the control panel. At the end of the morning Dr. Hugo turned in my direction, gave me one long piercing look, then without a word swept out of the room.

It didn't matter how much Mrs. L. consoled me, saying, "Everyone does it dearie! You'll be fine tomorrow." I still went home to spend a sleepless night convinced I would be told to leave the next day.

To their credit the higher beings allowed me a second chance and although I became much faster at cassette changing, I always touched the clips to reassure myself that the film was fixed in the right way round. Eventually I learnt all the necessary skills, including exposure technique, to manage a successful screening session without Letitia. And yes, I was unqualified too!

In today's world it would be unthinkable for two totally unqualified members of staff to perform these duties but somehow this situation suited everyone. All credit to Letitia, who in spite of her haughty manner, knew her job inside out.

The more exacting and eventful screening work took place in the afternoon. Again Dr. Hugo undertook most of these sessions with only addition to his protective apparel, a large pair of white rubber boots. Afternoon patient numbers were restricted to two as this matched the number of toilets and equipment available.

The next area of the digestive system under investigation, for tumours, blockages, inflammatory conditions such as ulcerative colitis and diverticula disease (small pouches developing in the intestinal wall) was the large bowel, using an examination known as Barium Enema, where the flow of barium was sent under pressure from the bottom up!

This method of assessing the large bowel involved diplomacy and patient care of the highest order. *(I never cease to marvel how people today willingly succumb to colonic irrigation as a health panacea, after assisting with barium enema examinations.)*

The means of administering the barium involved a three pint glass cylinder, three-quarters full of the warmed, diluted barium sulphate liquid, suspended from a drip stand. The height of the fluid could then be adjusted to increase or decrease the pressure of the flow down a long connecting tube into the large bowel, through a rubber balloon catheter inserted into the patient's anus. After much tuition from Letitia, it took me some while to pluck up enough courage to powder my hands, put on tight rubber gloves then separate the cheeks of an anxious human bottom; next insert a catheter into the appropriate orifice.

This deflated, bunchy piece of rubber tubing was lightly greased with a lubricating jelly, then with the patient lying on their left side, knees drawn up towards their chest, letting the x-ray gown fall apart to reveal a pink smooth or very hairy posterior, the deed was done. It was a straight forward procedure with male patients, but oh dear, the very possibility of tube insertion into the wrong opening for ladies incited me with a dire lack of confidence. Once correctly "in-situ" the catheter balloon was pumped up, supposedly to ensure it remained in position. In all cases, too much jelly and the catheter was expelled with great force, even when fully blown up! Hopefully if this occurred it would be before barium had flowed in, but it was not unknown to happen with the accompanying three pints of barium ejected explosively, spoutlike, all over the radiologist's feet; hence the white rubber boots! This time I felt sure the patient preferred the anonymity of the darkened room for their fifteen to twenty minutes ordeal.

Once the barium had been successfully pushed round to the last part of the large bowel, with following puffs of air encouraging the liquid to reach the end (called the caecum) and all the spot films taken, it was time to reverse the flow. The glass cylinder was lowered to floor level below the patient and with great relief much of the barium was siphoned off. At this point Dr. Hugo departed to his office and with great haste we removed all the plumbing, made our poor patient decent and almost ran with them to the loo, dripping a pathway of white blobs along the wooden floor. Mops and buckets were also vital pieces of equipment.

Thank goodness for the British "stiff upper lip" or ribald sense of humour because either attitude proved the saviour of our patients' dignity. Much to my relief I never recognised these people around Elmbridge as my whole attention had been directed to their nether regions.

The screening room was fully booked for action every weekday but the waiting lists remained at ten weeks or more. I spent four weeks learning to become of use during these procedures, gaining a great respect for Letitia, who succeeded in portraying this occupation, as one deemed, "magnificently desirable". A trooper of the first order!

Technology advances over the years have rendered these archaic methods obsolete. Barium procedures now take place in lit rooms, radiation has been minimised and although Barium Sulphate, still has to be ingested, these examinations take a fraction of the time in comparison to the old routines, so do not despair should you face such an investigation, there is nothing to fear!

Chapter 8

In November 1962 the "School of Radiography" officially opened with its first student; her name was Elizabeth. She was tall, my height but where I was plain and skinny she was curvaceous with long auburn hair and oozed confidence. Sister Aster was thrilled; here was a student to be proud of.

Elizabeth was a delightful person; with her open and friendly disposition she appeared to enjoy every aspect of her life. Her complexion radiated with a healthy glow and sprinkled golden, freckles spoke of previously enjoying an outdoor life; all that was about to change as she embarked on her hospital career, which would take place in the deepest region away from natural light. She had decided to take this opportunity to leave her family home and become an independent young woman, if she managed to pair up with a young doctor that would be a huge bonus. Her generous personality warmed her to everyone so it was no surprise that as new girls we quickly became friends.

The partnership formed between Elmbridge Hospital and the much larger model Brunswick General, twenty miles away in the neighbouring county, made the joint opening of a radiographic school more viable. It was intended for practical tuition to take place on site in each department, whereas theoretical training in lecture form would be given weekly, only at Brunswick. Further periods of study offered as tutorials, for our students, would be taken in Elmbridge by Mr. Petrie.

Elizabeth's family home was fifty miles away so she became a resident at the nurses' home under the watchful eye of Home Sister. I often took my lunch breaks with Anna at the Nurses' Home dining room and had discovered a radiographers' sitting room nearby. It was warmly carpeted, furnished with comfortable sofas, a bookcase filled with novels (rather than academic literature), bearing several ash-trays, along with a spindly spider-plant, loitering on its shelving. Floral curtains heavily perfumed with a musky, smoky scent, hung framing the windows. These overlooked a dingy, prefabricated building that housed the medical secretaries' office. Unfortunately my lowly status excluded me from experiencing such a comfortable spot; after lunch, if I had any spare minutes to fill, I had to return to the cramped department tearoom. It was here that Elizabeth's tutorials took place; sessions with Mr. Petrie that she began to dread but with no way of knowing how to avoid them? After three sessions, where he had struggled to complete any coherent sentences, she had had enough. She confided her dilemma to Martin, who agreed to help.

Within five minutes of Mr. Petrie's arrival at the next tutorial, his pager resounded urgently. He rushed along the Nurse's Home corridor in search of a phone, but the nearest was in Home Sister's office. He apologised, as Home Sister looked up, irritated by his intrusion, and called the department, only to find nobody had tried to get him. He returned to Elizabeth to continue his teaching, but immediately the pager set off again.

Home Sister's reception this time was decidedly frosty. "I think Mr. Petrie you are obviously required somewhere else, be so kind as to depart my office and return to your department forthwith. This is a home in which my nurses should be able to relax, not a public telephone exchange!"

Poor man his face flushed bright crimson; he had no way of dealing with her cold sarcasm. Stumbling from her office he poked his head around the sitting room door and stuttered to the surprised, but delighted Elizabeth, " I have to go…if..if…you need me….can you catch me….back….sorry!" and fled: he never braved the Nurses' Home again, instead he set and marked questions for Elizabeth, which proved a much more constructive use of both their time.

Elizabeth was two years my senior, not only did I envy her social skills but also her ability to make mistakes without hours of remorse, just acknowledging with good humour, whatever error she had made, then pressing on. Sister Aster was always gracious whenever Elizabeth erred whilst I was still severely admonished. This student's success was too important to the department's new status as a "School" for her to be demonised. In spite of her favoured treatment I never resented Elizabeth; she embodied my eagerly awaited role, a treasured student placement next October 1963.

Student Radiographers could follow two separate disciplines either diagnostic as our department practised or therapeutic radiography, which was the treatment undertaken by our therapy colleagues, to try to reduce or remove malignant tumours by radiation.

The Society of Radiographers had been founded as early as 1920 but Therapy Radiography did not get its own accreditation until 1947, in those early days students could qualify in both areas. Now it was considered that these professions were too complex to combine teaching of both within two years so all students only shared the first year of tuition. This initial course was necessary for both disciplines as each required proficiency in Physics, Hospital Practice and Anatomy. After the first part-one examination had been successfully completed the choice between diagnostic and therapy had to be made.

Neither Elizabeth nor I could envisage a career as a therapy radiographer but we had the greatest respect for those that did. They coped with the saddest situations, dealing with terminal illness every day, for in 1962 it was very rare for a patient with any of the multiple cancer diseases to achieve remission or survive five years from the initial diagnosis. Patients made frequent visits to the radiotherapy department and became well known to all the staff, who had to watch their charges decline over the weeks or months that followed. These radiotherapy radiographers required an inner strength to face the diminishing spirits and wasting bodies of their patients. We found it hard enough when such people returned, for regular chest x-rays, only to find they were losing their battle.

One such patient greatly affected us both as we struggled to achieve the right degree of professional detachment.

Rachel was nineteen years old and had become engaged to her childhood sweetheart six months before becoming ill. Her family attributed her sudden weight loss and extreme tiredness to her excitement in planning for her wedding arranged for the spring, next year. Tonics were taken, extra vitamin tablets and "early to bed" nights prescribed but all with no avail. Eventually her anxious mother managed to persuade Rachel to have a check-up with their G.P. His examination revealed her wasting body with large marbles of glands bulging under the angles of her chin; he acted immediately seeking an urgent hospital referral with one of the radiotherapy physicians. At that appointment her blood was taken for testing, along with a chest x-ray, where those combined results confirmed Hodgkin's disease to be the cause of her decline; her diagnosis was sealed.

This condition, (medically known as Lymph adenoma) was named after Thomas Hodgkin, who recognised malignant developments in the lymphatic system, which caused enlarged glands in the neck and other areas of the body. The liver and spleen would later become involved and towards the latter stages both lungs would slowly fill up with water, pushing the air capacity smaller and smaller until breathing became extremely distressed. This disease tended to affect young adults and in 1962 usually proved fatal.

Rachel was then treated with every available weapon to halt the malignant progress in her lymphatic system. She bore with great resilience many radiotherapy treatments, which bought her a few extra weeks and then suffered the latest weapon, in its early development, chemotherapy. This was the use of cytotoxic drugs, such as nitrogen mustard but sadly this treatment also only added to her wretchedness. Her weight plummeted further, her hair became thinner and scarcer as clumps fell from her scalp leaving her enormous, beautiful blue eyes naked of eyebrows or lashes, there was to be no respite.

Rachel knew she was seriously ill but at that time true knowledge was kept hidden from most patients; all medical notes and correspondence were written in a coded short-hand and no member of staff would have deemed it proper to tell her the truth. This was already a contentious issue, hotly debated at all levels of health care as unrealistic promises of recovery were still being delivered to terminally ill patients. Elizabeth and I saw her often, for her regular chest x-ray check as she was now an in-patient. We watched her grow weaker, her bubbly personality washing away with the precious pounds of weight she could ill afford to lose.

Her last visit was particularly poignant. Elizabeth was learning the technique for chest x-ray and as Rachel needed physical support to move from her wheel-chair to the carefully placed stool in front of the x-ray plate, Elizabeth called for me to help.

We gently unwrapped her from the softness of several blankets and started to remove her dressing gown.

"Wait ....I have something... to show you ....both," Rachel managed as she struggled for breath and from her pocket she pulled a carefully folded piece of paper. I took it and smoothed out a picture advertising a beautiful wedding dress. "It's crepe.... broderie anglais...on those lovely...trumpet sleeves....and a long train with more on...at the back," she wheezed with a beaming smile that lit up her yellow tinged skin.

"It's so beautiful Rachel," I replied "and from Bourne & Hollingsworth, Oxford Street no less!"

Elizabeth gazed approvingly at the advertisement and folded it carefully as she returned the paper to Rachel's pocket.

"Now shall I take your chain off or do you want to hold it in your teeth so that it's out of the way of your chest for the film?" asked Elizabeth, knowing how reluctant Rachel was to remove it, as her engagement ring, now too big for her pale wasted fingers, hung symbolically as close to her heart as was possible.

"No don't…. take it off…. please. I can …manage." Breathing was a great effort but with her precious chain still around her, hanging from the palest of lips, she held still, holding her breath, while the film was taken.

It was technically perfect but medically ruinous as so little air-filled lung tissue remained above the effusion of fluid, which grew bigger, relentlessly, everyday, slowly drowning this beautiful young woman.

We wrapped her back snugly in all her blankets, thanking her for showing us the beautiful dress she had chosen.

As she was wheeled out of the department she glanced back at us and said, "Pink roses…. and lily of the valley… for my bouquet."

Within the week she died and placed on top of her funeral coffin rested her sweetly scented dream bouquet, with blooms of pink and white.

I think now perhaps it was right to leave her in her wedding dream, surely that was kinder than removing all hope, leaving total despair, for she had been just one year older than Ellen and three years older than me. How unjust was that! The day we learnt Rachel had died, Elizabeth and I missed lunch and went for a walk. Free of the constraints of the department we shed our tears, hugging each other, knowing this would be the first of many encounters with the unfair choices made by the "Angel of Death."

Chapter 9

Sister Aster decided it was possibly safe to allocate me to Stuart for training in the huge responsibility that was the darkroom. I viewed this with a mixture of excitement and apprehension as I knew within the processing procedures all manner of hazards lurked ready to cause my downfall. The chemical processes of developing a radiograph seemed mystical. A thin, pale green, coated sheet of paper-like material had to be immersed in several tanks of liquids to emerge totally transformed bearing a glossy black and white negative image, which could be viewed from both sides to reveal the intricate structure of our inner selves.

Stuart was an amiable, fresh faced fellow recently reaching twenty, stocky, calm, just the right temperament to deal with the constant crashing of exposed films into the darkroom hatches and the impatient door bashing from radiographers demanding to see their developed films immediately. Nothing seemed to ruffle his composure but I feared a major travesty on my part might unleash a hither to unknown torrent of rage.

The actual darkroom consisted of a small area about twelve feet by eight with a working bench attached on its longest side opposite the locked door. Above this bench to the left was the main hatch directly linking through to the general x-ray room, Room 2. It had a double cavity, where on one side was held various sizes of unexposed cassettes frequently used for chest, back, skull and limb examinations. The other side of the divide had a loose bottom floor so that when exposed cassettes were placed on it, along with an identifying strip of patient-named and dated paper, their pressure triggered a red light to be switched on in the darkroom, alerting Stuart, just in case he had failed to hear the clattering entry of several thin metal cassettes with their exposed films.

The darkroom's endless streams of films were not sensitive to the soft red glow emitted from its four safe lights so that after several minutes eyes became adjusted to working in this bordello lit atmosphere, hence its sniggering reputation throughout the hospital. Under the bench was a spring-loaded hopper containing the most popular sizes of unexposed films for re-loading the vacated cassettes. It was a vicious beast trapping any finger that failed to retract quickly enough but designed to shut speedily in case any white light erroneously crept into the darkroom. Along the shorter wall, adjacent to the door, stood a large water filled tank kept at a constantly warm temperature. Free standing within it (so they could be removed for the arduous, smelly task of cleaning) was the four processing tanks. First, surrounded by its warm water blanket, directly under three timing devices, stood the developing chemical tank, next a small, immediate rinse tank of agitated water, followed by two separate fixing chemical tanks.

This whole wet area, concealed in its dampness, several families of cockroaches, who ventured out at night, when it was quiet, to torment the on-call, duty radiographer. Often the night porter was summoned to stamp his size 13 feet to send them scurrying back under the tanks, but even then it felt creepy knowing of their hidden presence.

The darkroom door was kept locked while processing took place, however using a light-tight, pass through hatch, the processed films were pushed out into the wet viewing room with its numerous light boxes and the hot, noisy drying cabinet.

Any lull in production rendered the darkroom door thrown open with delight to rejoin the living from this dark, airless, chemically infused other-world.

The viewing room was the hub of the department, where anxious, impatient radiographers grabbed their respective films to check for technical accuracy.

Was the position right? Was the film too dark or too light, too grey or too "contrasty?"

Was it crisp, sharp or had the bugger moved, shaken or breathed, blurring the image?

Could you see the anatomical bit the doctor asked for?!!

Many an expletive was uttered under the breath regardless of the proximity of the patient changing cubicles and in truth Martin could often be heard at the reception desk!

This was to be my base for the next two months; a world within a world.

The greatest hazards I faced was either "fogging" a film after exposure by somehow allowing white light to hit the emulsion surface of the film and destroying the image or fogging it pre-exposure so making it completely grey or totally black and useless to the unsuspecting radiographer about to use it.

I knew they were disasters in waiting and the worry kept me awake for the first few nights of my secondment.

Stuart was admired and respected by the radiographers because he had achieved a great skill in "watching" films during development. If he saw a film developing too quickly so that the image may become too black, he ignored the set timer and whipped the radiograph out early, placing it swiftly into the rinse, then the fixer. Although the quality might be reduced by under-development often the result was diagnostic and stopped any need to repeat the dosage of radiation with another exposure. Extremely precious images such as pregnancy films especially benefitted from his watchful eye.

Although diagnostic ultrasound had been pioneered in medicine in 1958 by Professor Donald, its use in maternity scanning was a long way off so in 1962 there were no diagnostic ultrasound techniques to monitor pregnancy and the developing foetus. Although current knowledge recognised the harmful effects of radiation, only x-rays could fulfil the necessary role of providing vital information about the safety of mother and baby.

It was essential to know, (if possible before labour began, even sometimes during labour,) whether a mother's pelvis was roomy enough for a normal delivery, how many babies there were, what the position of that baby was, head first or breech?

All questions the Obstetrician needed to have answered, along with more spine-chilling requests to determine whether the baby was malformed.

Only an x-ray could prepare the doctors and midwives for any possible complications.

A once only x-ray shot was essential, usually taken by the most experienced radiographer available. Then the film would be rushed to the darkroom with "Pregnancy watch it Stuart!" called as it was cluttered into the hatch. Stuart aimed to present the perfect picture, which would identify the tiny bone structure of a miniature human being, curled up ready, waiting to be born from the abdomen of another human being.

Where more than one baby shared that limited space the films were amazing to see; the babies' heads, spines and limbs could all be unscrambled from their mother's pelvic bones. Tiny hands and fingers were shown sometimes even sucking their thumbs as a digit could be picked out between the white spots of milk-teeth erupting from the jaws. One question could not be answered however, which gender was the foetus?

The genitals consisted of soft tissue and did not cast any shadows onto x-ray film so at that time the mystery of which sex remained.

In these multiple births of twins and triplets (I never saw quadruplets) we counted the heads first, then usually followed each spine accurately but limbs proved more difficult as they often became entwined, perhaps dancing or already embarking on sibling rivalry and having a tussle to see who would be the most senior and first out.

Such magical images never ceased to fill me with wonder at the complex structure of developing human beings cocooned within their heavily laden mothers.

There was one other pregnancy film occasionally requested, that was to determine in the first few weeks, as to whether a baby had been conceived.

One afternoon Jeanette knocked on the darkroom door, "Stuart, I need a quiet word please." Stuart raised his eyebrows to me wondering what the problem was. As soon as it was safe to let daylight in he opened the door.

"How can I help?" he asked.

"I have a young patient, Betty Shaw, she's only 13 years old, for a pelvis film. We are looking for signs of an early pregnancy, possibly 13 or 14 weeks, so something should show on the film."

Again with no ultrasound available, a pelvic film at 12-14 weeks could reveal early bone structure, but at this stage x-rays were potentially very harmful to the baby so it was an investigation performed as a last resort.

"I can only take one picture, you do appreciate that don't you?" she added. Jeanette knew there would be no room for error.

"It'll be fine, trust us." Stuart reassured her confidently.

I peeked out from the wet-viewing room to catch sight of a young teenager, who looked far too small to have a baby. Her fair hair was gathered in bunches and a flash of metal from her mouth revealed braces, caging her teeth, as she spoke to Jeanette. The Senior Radiographer placed a protective arm around Betty and steered her into Room 2.

Several minutes later a film cassette clattered into the hatch, its flashing red light blazing us into action. True to his word, Stuart checked its progress through the developer until satisfied it had reached perfection.

Once fixed he brought it out to Jeanette, who studied the film closely against the light-box for some time, before pointing to me a tiny almost translucent skull bone, "Do you see those little white marks as well? They are rudimentary limbs. She is definitely pregnant! About 14 weeks I reckon. I am going to take it round to Dr. Weston-Smythe for an urgent report."

The radiologist confirmed all that Jeanette had said to Betty's GP, he would have the difficult task of helping her through to the baby's birth.

There would be no termination; instead a baby born to a young girl who had barely left childhood behind. Who was the father? Well most probably a relative, grandfather, uncle or even her own dad for that sort of incestuous abuse would always exist. Betty faced a tough time ahead especially after giving birth because her baby, who would be taken from her and adopted, could never know his young mother and the trauma she had gone through to give him life. In addition Betty would be branded "a sinful unmarried mother" for a very long time.

There was one other tiny darkroom in the hospital, a converted cupboard transformed for developing films next to the operating theatres. Once a radiographer was gowned-up, booted and wearing a head covering and mask the last thing he or she needed was to return to the department to develop her film, only to go through the whole dressing up performance again. To speed up delivery of the radiograph during surgery this basic developing unit had been brought together. Two small tanks stood side by side containing the requisite chemicals with a water rinse between them. Hangers and boxes of unexposed films made up the remaining equipment for an almost instant film to be offered up to the surgeon.

Several types of operations benefitted from immediate x-rays: pinning and plating of fractured hips, removing gall-bladders and checking for free flowing bile ducts, searching for missing instruments or swabs and any number of cautionary checks. It was stressful work so being in control of developing one's own film was a bonus. All radiographers had to become masters of wet developing; on-call duty at night was a solitary experience, requiring knowledge of all the daytime back-up skills, out of hours.

Thus it was necessary for the final year lectures and examination papers to cover all the theoretical aspects of x-ray photography, so for me to have this opportunity as a cadet nurse, would give me a huge boost towards future student radiography accomplishments.

I watched Stuart, when my eyes were adapted to the red glow that enveloped us as he instructed me stage by stage in how to access and prepare a film for development.

"You open the cassette at the clips like this but there are at least four various designs of openings in use, I will have to show you each one as we meet them."

"Stuart, what's that scratching noise?" I asked him.

"I can't hear anything! Next you gently slide the film out from the cassette, touch it as little as possible, reach up and take down the appropriate sized hanger then grip the four corners of the film with each of its clasps so that it is totally supported" (I had of course unloaded these hangers in the wet-room in daylight to put the film into the drying cabinet so no worries there).

"Stuart, there it is again!"

"Yes, OK, I heard that; let me put the developer lid back on, then we can switch on the white lights."

He submerged the film under the liquid, resting the top outer edges of the frame on the exposed ledges and set the timer to three minutes; then with the lid safely in place he turned on the lights, to come face to face with a large rat.

"Oh God!" I yelled and swung myself up onto the workbench, while for a few moments Stuart froze.

"Right you stay there I will get Ted to sort this out!"

"No you're not leaving me in here with that!" I wailed.

"Yes I am. He must have come in through the outlet pipe. If we open the door too much he will escape out into the department," he replied, gingerly pulling back the lock and carefully sliding around the smallest gap, as he firmly shut the door behind him.

At that point the timer rang to announce the film was "cooked" and needed to come out of the developer.

"Oh no! I've got to turn off the white light, get to the switch, and take the film out, else it will be ruined," I muttered angrily. How could he leave me like this! I grabbed a large hanger and reaching across the darkroom pushed it hard against the switch. After three attempts, I managed to click the switch off as it plunged the room back into its usual red glow.

I could just reach the developing tanks lying on my tummy, with my head and shoulders overhanging the bench, to haul the film out, dripping developer everywhere. Next I managed to give it a quick splash in the rinse and then tossed it into the fixer. Thankfully it clunked to the bottom of the tank.

In my panic I had almost forgotten about the rat.

The darkroom door, gently opened, as Ted and Stuart slipped back in.

"Why are we in darkness?" Stuart asked.

"Cos I had to take the film out of the developer."

"Blast, I forgot all about that one. Well done Mary, great stuff," praise indeed from Stuart. The lights went on to reveal Ted carrying a large snow shovel.

Stuart leapt up on the bench beside me, while Ted approached the rat, slinking in the corner by the film hopper, cutting him off from any escape. Wallop! He brought the curved metal plate down as hard as he could and flattened the creature in one mighty blow. I jumped down and rushed out into the wet room, not wanting to see what mangled mess the killing had made. Coffee, that's what I needed and a chance to tell the tale!

To my surprise and pleasure, by rescuing the developing film in the presence of a *huge* rat (that grew with every rendition), I became the hero of the hour, with even a kind word from Sister Aster. From then on I was trusted to "stand-in" for Stuart during his break times; the darkroom secondment had been a success.

.

Chapter 10

Just after Christmas the hospital held its annual dinner and dance in the town's most prestigious hotel, which provided a large ballroom for the occasion. Consultants, Junior Doctors, Sisters, Student Nurses, Nursing Auxiliaries, Pathology Technicians, Physiotherapists, Radiographers, Cleaning Staff and Porters, everyone was invited.

I was excited at this opportunity to shed my schoolgirl image in front of my work colleagues, choosing to wear a red top and black mini-skirt, along with sophisticated, black patent leather shoes with 3-inch stiletto heels! Why not? After all no one would be asking me to dance.

Two previous days of heavy snow had left the roads ingrained with crisply raised, frozen, grey patterned, tyre tracks, criss-crossing each other, framed by white snow castles all along the gutters. Daphne was getting a lift with us and promised to 'keep an eye on me.'

Dad drove carefully as conditions worsened and dropped both of us at the hotel at 7.30pm. "Now Mary, be sure to catch the last bus home, there is more snow forecast for later tonight and I want you home before it comes. Do you hear me!" he insisted.

"Yes, yes Dad!" I replied impatiently.

"Thanks for the lift," we both chimed, eager to be free and head off for the festivities.

The bright lights and sudden warmth steamed up our respective glasses as we climbed the stairs of the hotel to join the throng.

"See you later Mary. I shall probably go on to Lucinda's afterwards, she's planning a party where we can really let our hair down. You can come too if you want," she gave me a wave then disappeared to find her set of friends, which included Lucinda, also a third year student nurse.

I quickly found the table, where some of the x-ray department staff, Ted, Mrs L. Brenda and Stella and some of the others were gathered. I found an empty seat and sat down next to Elizabeth. She looked gorgeous, a shimmering green dress, setting off her long auburn curls. I hoped I looked more confident than I felt, hiding the nervous fluttering stirring in my stomach, with the sophistication of a cigarette between my fingers. After nearly five months the medical habit of smoking had caught me in its trap.

Now it seems bizarre, but the heaviest social smokers appeared to be from the medical profession, Doctors from consultant down, senior nurses to juniors and now cadets were soothed by lighting up this fashionable pacifier and exhaling the smoke, trying to emulate the nonchalant style of a film star. I smoked the popular, cheap cigarettes "Embassy" to save their coupons, for some trinket or other. Occasionally, I indulged in an exotic Balkan Sobrani, wafting the black leaf, scented aroma around as it burned, hopefully displaying myself as the epitome of sophistication but at an unaffordable price. Mrs. L, Stella and I stubbed out our cigarettes and unfolded crisp, white napkins as dinner was about to be served. We had already studied the exotic menu, well that's what it seemed to me, which boasted:

Starter	*Prawn Cocktail*
Main Course	*Coq au Vin*
Desert	*Black Forest Gateau*
To follow	*Coffee & After Eight*

Mints.

At that moment we all glanced up to see Letitia, looking our way with a very self-satisfied smile, arriving arm in arm with Dr. Meredith as they made their way to the Junior Doctor's table.

"Oh! Just our luck, she's snared her prey, we shall never hear the last of that," groaned Stella to everyone's agreement. But to my greater surprise, Sister Aster walked in escorted by Dr. Patterson, so perhaps there was some truth to the romantic rumours I'd heard after all. This evening was proving to be a revelation; even Home Sister was behaving quite "kittenish" with Mr. Kerrigan, in whose buttonhole rested a pure white rose. She was wearing a shiny blue-shot, ankle length, taffeta skirt, supported by layers of net petticoats and a pale blue, satin blouse. In her hand, she clutched tightly, what appeared to be, a large glass of bitter lemon.

Mrs. L. nudged me chuckling in my ear, "That's got a hearty measure of gin in it, Mary. Look she's a bit tipsy already." Sure enough her pink face and unsteady manner was beginning to attract a great deal of attention.

The band struck up as soon as the meal was over and the specially sprung dance floor vibrated with Quick-Steps and Cha-Cha-Chas. Suddenly Home-Sister took to the floor, hoisted her skirt and petticoats "Can-Can" style, flashing a red pair of long-johns to all of us still seated and twirled enthusiastically round and round. The band responded, launching into Offenbach's familiar music, while she plucked the rose from an astonished Mr. Kerrigan's jacket and placed it between her teeth. Everyone stood up, clapping to the rhythm of the beat, cheering her on as she tossed her skirt back and forth spinning round. The bright lights caught the white rose flashing from her teeth, when suddenly she twirled too far, colliding with an occupied table, which sent their bottle of wine crashing to the floor.

Mr. Kerrigan and Dr. Patterson sprang into action, grabbing her by the arms, as they quickly lead this drunk, dazed, dancer away from the limelight and downstairs, where Sister Aster draped a full-length cloak around her shoulder's ready for a quick departure.

Next morning Home Sister was nowhere to be seen; however a brief note from Matron, reported that Home Sister's soft drinks had been tampered with by some unscrupulous person, determined to make her look foolish and that Matron would not rest until the perpetrator had been caught. This whole escapade was never mentioned again.

In truth she had been the highlight of the evening and for once had almost appeared human.

As we returned to our table, after all that excitement, Elizabeth's cheeks flushed and her eyes brightened, watching young Dr. Sayeed Ahmed, the Medical Houseman, making his way towards her. I knew she was "keen" on him, so for her the evening was proving successful already. He took her arm, steering her onto the dance floor, where they made a very attractive couple, and that was the last sight I had of her for the rest of the evening. Ted came over and rescued me for a waltz, with his wife's approval, but after that, the role of "wall-flower" fell to me. The evening had fallen flat, rather as I had expected, so I was quite relieved when the time came round for my last bus.

Just as I was preparing to leave, Daphne sought me out, "Come on, let's get you to Lucinda's party and loosen you up a bit. Honestly Mary you look like a stuffed prune!" she said, not unkindly.

"Well, I'll be for the high jump if I'm late, you heard Dad," I replied.

"Oh! Too bad; let your hair down, live a bit. Come on we're off now!" She grabbed my arm as I flashed a grateful smile at her; I knew she was trying her best to help me mix in with her nursing set and have a good time.

Still anxious I said, "Thanks, but we won't be too late will we?"

"No, no, now do stop worrying and come on!" She urged impatiently.

Stepping outside was a shock, for there was more snow, falling heavily, muffling the shouts coming from the gathered group of about twenty people, who were walking the short distance to Lucinda's house. Her parents had not yet returned home from their Christmas cruise, leaving their three storey town house perfectly empty for one of Lucinda's famous parties.

My 3-inch stiletto heeled shoes, slipped and slithered on the icy surface as we headed off to Lucinda's home. Once inside couples paired off in all directions and those not spoken for seemed to grab whoever of the opposite sex was nearest.

All the lights were extinguished, whilst giggles, screeches and yells permeated the rooms. To my amazement, I was grabbed by a young male nurse, who was just as inexperienced as me, no doubt the reason he had chosen me. Our combined sexual activity or knowledge appeared to be "snogging."

Well, OK I could handle that!

I had promised my parents that I would be home by that last bus, but when I finally caught a glimpse of my watch from the street-lamp outside it read 1.15 am. Oh my God, Dad would kill me! There was no sign of Daphne and my slippery, lipped partner had disappeared to the loo, so I fumbled through the coats, clutched mine with relief, then grabbing bag and shoes dashed to the door. A strange pair of male hands tried to pull me down by the waist, but my panic was so great I kicked at him hard and barged, breathlessly, out of the house. The relief I had felt at escaping was quickly forgotten when I looked about me.

I knew the way home but the depth of snow shook me, I had two miles to walk in those stupid heeled shoes, already soaking wet and chafing with every step.

No one knew then, that this winter of 1962 into1963 would later prove to be one of the coldest recorded, even more so than the bitter weather experienced in 1947. No wonder I was colder than I had ever been, and wet through with blistered feet. I tried to hurry, but slithered and slipped, ricking my ankles on the crusty, iced snow rucks. It would take me hours to walk home along these silent, ghostly, lit streets. The beams from the street lamps became mottled with snowflake shadows, a muffled car engine vibrated in the distance, but I seemed to be the only living being, freezing and shivering outside the warmth of a home. Then, turning a corner I saw skewed to one side, pointing towards a pillar-box, a car caught in a snowdrift. Getting closer, to my joy, it was Dad.

"Oh! Thank goodness,' I shouted, my voice echoing eerily in the frozen air, "Dad, it's me!"

"Where the hell have you been? We've been worried sick. I've spent hours driving up and down in these conditions trying to find you and now I'm stuck!" his rage was palpable, but I didn't care, here was my saviour.

"I went back to Lucinda's for coffee with Daphne. I didn't want to come home alone, but in the end it was so late I knew I had to get back. Dad I'm truly sorry!"

"I went passed her house but it was in darkness, no sign of life at all," he seethed.

Thank God he hadn't called I thought.

"We were round the back," I lied despondently.

He was rightfully furious and I knew I would suffer his wrath in the morning, but now our priority was to free the car. Being Dad, like any boy scout he had come out prepared. He handed me some old sacking to place directly behind the car's wheels, while he retrieved a shovel from the boot and we dug away at the snow. After several attempts, he managed to reverse the car so that the wheels gripped on the sacking and drive it into the middle of the road. Then in the highest gear possible we crawled our way home in total silence. He opened the door without a word, for at the top of the stairs stood Mum, her ghastly pallor reflected how dreadful their fears for my safety had been.

"Get to bed," he ordered.

Through my self-centered misery I knew the whole evening had been a disaster; one I wanted to forget but for just that reason I never did.

When Daphne got to hear of my father's reaction the following day and suffered her own father's (my uncle's) chastisement for "leading me astray," she scornfully rejected me as far too immature to be included in her set. And do you know I was gratefully relieved.

I loved the music, I loved the fashions but the sexual freedom offered by the swinging sixties would have to wait for me to grow up; I truly was far too young to be liberated.

Chapter 11

The working atmosphere on our department was very sociable with a family feel which owed much to the motherly affection shown to all by Mrs. Lewis. Although her status was only that of a nursing auxiliary, she was loved and respected by everyone. She was a comely lady in her late forties eagerly awaiting the marriage of her only daughter Susan.

Mrs. L. was a "Yorkshire lass," who had grown up in Huntington situated on the outskirts of the historic town of York. She had left school at fifteen, to be employed by Timothy White's, a hard-wear store, which had branches all over the country.

When Mrs. L. was sixteen, she met her future husband, George, at the local church youth club. He was one year older and they started to "go steady," each happy and content with their choice of partner.

George was looking for a good electrical apprenticeship, so he was delighted to be accepted, by a company that made electrical components in Elmbridge. It meant a move south, away from friends and family. She was now seventeen and George eighteen, but young as they were, their confidence in each other was unbreakable and they were determined not to be separated, deciding on a small family wedding in the church where they had first met. Then Mr. and Mrs. Lewis made their way south to begin their married life.

Mrs L. was taken on immediately by Timothy Whites in Elmbridge, working full-time until George qualified as an electrician. Boosted by his increase in wages they decided at last it was time to start their longed for family. It wasn't as easy as they had hoped. Mrs. L. had two miscarriages and had to wait three long years before Susan was born. Sadly there were to be no siblings for her, so all their nurturing love was poured into their only daughter.

Susan was now twenty-four and eagerly planning her wedding, a date had been chosen and the expected highlight of Mrs. L's life fixed for six months time. We all enjoyed hearing about the search for her apparel, bride's and bridesmaids' dresses, colour schemes and all the accompanying paraphernalia that engulfed a wedding. Her lilac veiled hat had been brought in for approval and Martin's modelling of it gave her great delight. Such pleasure and excitement was a tonic when some days could be heavy with human frailty and serious trauma.

Early one Thursday morning just after I had arrived in the department, I nipped into the staff room to drink my usual cuppa with Mrs L., Connie, Ted and Stella; a habit I had got into from my first day, sharing their news and any gossip.

"Are you OK Mrs. L?" I asked her anxiously as she looked pale and strained.

"I've got a bit of face ache dear," she responded, "don't look so worried dear, I'll ask Martin for some aspirin when he comes in," and with that she trotted off, gingerly massaging her cheek and jaw with her right hand.

Later on that morning I caught Martin saying, "You go off sick Mrs. L., take some more aspirin when you get home and tuck yourself in bed for a sleep. I'll fix it with Mr. French, the dental surgeon to see you in his clinic tomorrow, he'll soon have it sorted out."

Still in pain but looking relieved that she only had to wait for tomorrow, Mrs. L. left for her bike ride home.

The next morning Mrs. L arrived grey and weary, it was obvious that there had been no respite from this persistent pain. Mr. French referred her straight back to us for a series of dental x-rays. Martin took charge; no one else would be allowed to perform this task, sending her back to the clinic with the films as quickly as he could. After completing her consultation she reported back to an anxiously waiting group of staff, "There were no abscesses or infections shown on my x-rays. Mr. French is going to refer me to the neurologist; he thinks it's a nerve thingy, I'm going to see Mr. Lucas at his Monday afternoon clinic, so I'll see you all then. Cheerio!" then off she went but this time returning home by car, as George her husband had forbidden her from riding her bike, and taken a rare morning off to accompany and transport her.

Monday seemed an uneasy morning without her, but we waited hopeful that a restful weekend had brought her some relief. Not so, as she walked slowly into the department that afternoon we were appalled to see how she continued to be ravaged with pain. Her usual plump, rosy-cheeked face with its open smile was pale and pinched. Her eyes were deadened with painkillers, huge black rings encircled them, her gait was also unsteady as she came for her appointment, desperately seeking relief from this vice-like grip to her jaw and face.

Mr. Lucas also sent her straight back, this time for x-rays of her facial bones. His initial appraisal had included a possible diagnosis of trigeminal neuralgia, an extremely painful inflammation of that facial nerve; if correct this horrible condition would eventually subside, but as a precaution and to exclude other possibilities he had requested a technically difficult series of facial radiographs.

Martin once again took charge, he would let no one else in the room and when the examination was completed yelled through the hatch door to Stuart, "These are Mrs. L's films, watch them with your life!"

I truly believe the whole department held its breath. Martin's quick film check confirmed that all the films were of excellent quality, no rush stuff or cutting corners here. He quickly grabbed them out of sight and marched them to Dr. Weston-Smythe for a report, who personally wrote his report so that its substance was not divulged to either secretary or any other member of staff. Martin and Dr. Weston-Smythe were the only two departmental personnel to know what diagnosis he had been made.

They both strode off to Dr. Lucas' clinic, while Stella helped her dear friend along the corridor.

Martin returned grim-faced but not a word would he reveal, her privacy, as that of any other patient would prevail.

Two months went by and still Mrs. L was on sick leave. One by one we called to see her at home filling her in with gossip and chit chat. No one ventured to voice what we all feared, whilst the impending wedding drew ever closer. Instead of her infectious excitement now there was only the ordeal of pain. Its severity had never left her, shrinking her bustling figure to a wasted frame, wheel-chair bound as she became weaker by the day. One of my many cousins was a hairdresser who lived close by. Once a week she called in to wash, dry and set Mrs. L's hair, helping to keep her morale positive, but one week after her usual visit she called me at home. She was an emotionally strong girl but struggled through her tears to tell me she wouldn't be needed any more as Mrs. L. was now too weak to hold her head up.

At length this dear lady was admitted to the women's medical ward in the hospital she had served for so long, to a side room away from the noise and inevitable hustle and bustle. Her diagnosis remained shielded from her but she was barely conscious, hardly aware of her surroundings. Of course what we had all dreaded had become fact; she had an inoperable, fast-growing facial tumour, which had only become apparent when it enveloped the trigeminal nerve, hence the severe never-ending pain.

Susan's wedding plans struggled on, as they could ill-afford to forfeit the hefty deposits already placed for the venue, caterers and all the nuptial periphery; following all the time her mother's wishes, "Go ahead you'll see I'll be all right on the day, dearie!" until it was too late to change.

Instead of their planned joyous occasion the bride and groom went numbly through the required rituals, then after the service, still in full bridal regalia and attended by her three bridesmaids carrying their bouquets, Susan and her new husband framed Mrs. L's bedside. Did she know they were there? Who knows, but just two days later she died. It seemed to me, being Mrs. L and not wanting to cause a fuss or any delays, she had stayed around until they left for their honeymoon.

For several months the muted atmosphere in the department affected everyone. Laughter was rare and guilty, as we grieved our loss. The early morning cuppa sessions never resumed for there was no pleasure to be had without her cheery chit-chat.

Stella was upgraded to Mrs. L's position, her former role didn't need replacing, because recently, much equipment such as needles, syringes even vomit bowls had become disposable, arriving pre-packed and sterile from a central sterilising unit. To Stella's credit she filled her new position with ease and it was her perky attitude to life that finally cleared the clouds away, so that gradually we could let dear Mrs. L.'s memories give us pleasure and let her rest in peace.

I, too, was fast approaching a change of position; to my great delight the Hospital Management Committee had accepted my application to join the next student intake, which was due to begin in a few months time.

Mrs. L. would have beamed with approval. I never forgot how she showed kindness and compassion to everyone; she had set me a standard of care, which I determined to follow.

Part Two

Chapter 12

During February 1963, Sister Aster retired. I quite missed the clacking of her tiny footsteps tapping out behind me, for thankfully our relationship had improved considerably after Mrs. Lewis' illness, as if knowing I had no motherly protector rendered her sport too unfair and difficult for even her to justify. In fact she had strengthened my resolve to succeed in my chosen career with her earlier spiteful attitude, never again did I let myself be intimidated by impatient surgeons, aggressive old "battle-axed" nurses or pompous physicians. She had unwittingly performed a great service, forcing me to grow more self-confident and forcing me to grow up. Now at 17 years of age I was emotionally stronger, a much needed, attribute if I was to cope with badly injured, severely ill and sometimes very difficult patients.

The hospital management committee had decided to promote Mr. Petrie to the Superintendent Radiographer post, with Martin filling the Deputy position. Their decision to endorse Mr. Petrie in this position surprised many, but the three consultants, who wanted their own way in departmental issues, had considered him to be a "push-over," weak enough to sway and had persuaded the other members of the committee that he was "up to the job." However it was a decision they came to regret, for even in the first few months, Mr. Petrie showed a stubborn streak previously hidden. He was not open to persuasion, bribery or threats so if he didn't agree with ideas that didn't match his own, he simply shut out any discussion and retreated behind the closed doors of his office. It was impossible to argue with him.

This apparently quiet man was married with two children, but how any of these events had occurred was difficult to imagine. His hitherto communication problems with his staff increased, bringing about frustration and misunderstandings when he stuttered and stumbled through complex instructions. The morale of the department was suffering.

The person who suffered most from this unhappy situation was Martin. His pleasure at being promoted was short lived, as his gregarious personality clashed with the introverted nature of his superior, who failed to include him in any decision-making. Because Martin was so much more approachable, he was frequently hounded by the remaining staff anxious for explanations about changes in working practices suddenly introduced into the department. Unfortunately, being as ignorant as they were, he could give them no answers.

Martin became irritable, often missing from main x-ray, choosing to supervise the small

 X-ray facilities in those village hospitals encompassed by the Elmbridge group. That way he could avoid having to deal with a man who simply never listened.

Martin had a wide and interesting life outside the hospital. He played hockey in the winter and tennis in the summer belonging to several clubs. He was the popular chairman of one of Elmbridge's main charity groups, organising dances, the local carnival, firework night and a Christmas market, raising money for various good causes. Out of work he felt appreciated and during this difficult time these activities became more important. He was never short of female company, girlfriends came and went but he seemed to have no desire to settle down,

Perhaps he just hadn't found the right person.

Despite the general uneasiness with these changes, they mainly affected departmental administration and as the number of patients never relented, work had to go on, giving the people the best service possible. Little of this affected my cadetship, which I knew had proved invaluable. I was ready to start training. My first goal to become a student radiographer was finally within reach.

During the summer months, prospective students hoping to join me for the October in-take, arrived for interview and the required medical examinations. Tuberculosis still commanded a fearful presence and each person proposing to work in the hospital had a chest x-ray to eliminate the possibility of passing on this monstrous illness. The three prospective students selected to make up our quartet were: Linda, Joanna and Curtis. Although this was still a predominately female occupation, the introduction of more intricate equipment with the need to understand elements of radiation physics and much photography, had prompted increasing numbers of men to show interest.

The four of us were about to spend over two years constantly in each others company so it was vital that we could work well together, loyalty and friendship between us was the only way such a grouping would survive. We were also the first "group in-take" as Elizabeth, who was one year senior, was now shadowing radiographers whenever she was not studying, so it was deemed the success of our studentship would determine the future of Elmbridge School of Radiography; we were constantly reminded by Mr. Petrie of our collective responsibility.

My first positive impressions of my new contemporaries turned out to be mostly accurate. Although Linda seemed quiet with her gentle sense of humour, she proved to be emotionally strong and never waivered from any daunting sight or smell, in fact very often she became the most practical and just got on with the job in hand. She had been working in a laboratory since school, developing a sharp, analytic mind. Linda was petite, brunette with short, bobbed hair framing her pretty face, just the opposite to my fair headed, be-spectacled and gangling frame. We became friends immediately, although unknowing then, that this friendship would still be strong today.

Joanna was middle height with highlighted blonde hair twisted into the latest, stylish French pleat. She also wore glasses, favouring the current fashion of heavy, owlish black frames, conveying a studious image, which hid her sense of fun and quick-witted repartee. She travelled from north London every day by train, favouring the intimacy of our small general hospital to pursue her career, rather than one of the large city teaching hospitals. As a fellow Londoner we had much in common and enjoyed the same silly jokes so no problem there!

Curtis surprised us all. Amazingly this former Public Schoolboy and ex-cadet naval officer joined the three of us with ease. His lack of pomposity probably had derived from serving on a merchant ship, where any pretentions would have been severely dealt with by the crew.

He had originally set out from boarding school to become a navigating officer, in the merchant navy, but discovered that any prospect of a future, stable, family life seemed incompatible with this profession. His own childhood experience had been one devoid of consistent parental involvement, with both his mother and father working and living abroad. Sadly, while Curtis was at boarding school aged only nine, his father had died, prompting his mother to return to Elmbridge, find a home and support her family, thereby leaving her role as a Queen Alexander Nurse in Palestine.

Relieved to gain employment, she took the only part-time post available, as a visiting school nurse. It was even tougher then to live the life of a single, working mother, trying to balance financial necessity against managing a home and family. Curtis told us that once, many years previously, she had been the women's medical ward sister at Elmbridge, so with his family background he had found changing to a medical career an easy option.

On the day all three prospective students attended for their requisite chest x-rays, Martin instructed me to take them on a tour of the hospital, then finally to entertain them with coffee in the radiographers' sitting room at the Nurses' Home.

I lead them up the corridor towards the Casualty Department, confidently directing proceedings and feeling quite important in my crisp white uniform.

Of course, I should have known, that was folly indeed!

Just as we turned the corner towards Casualty's collection of rooms, the entrance doors were flung open by a large man clutching his right hand, draped in a bloody towel, above his head, as he crashed through blocking our path.

"Help me please!" he shouted, releasing his grip on his injured hand and grabbing me instead. "I got my hand caught in the lawn mower," he sobbed, whipping off the towel and thrusting four mangled finger stumps and a thumb dangling, all dripping in blood in my face.

Horrified I snatched the towel, quickly wrapping it back round this horrendous sight, as all four of us propelled him passed the reception desk, with several waiting patients open-mouthed, to the emergency cubicles beyond. Instantly Sister appeared to see what all the noise was about and calmly took over, sitting him down to assess his state of shock as well as his injury, while the three prospected students quietly retreated. Unsure what to do, I held my post until moments later Dr. Khan arrived and the two of them set to work to stem the flow of blood, still cascading to the floor. Sister looked up thanking me and signalled I was to leave them.

Still shocked and a little dazed, I had totally forgotten the others and the proposed tour, so looked in surprise to find them all waiting for me just outside in the corridor.

"Mary, you're uniform is covered in blood," Linda pointed out. "Come on show me where you change and we'll get you sorted."

She placed a comforting arm around my shaking shoulders as we walked over to the Nurses' Home. Curtis and Joanna set off to find the refectory bringing much needed coffee to the sitting room; together once again, we sank back on the comfortable chairs in reflective silence.

"Well!" I gasped, breaking the awkward hush, "You've certainly had an introduction to hospital life then. Are you sure you still want to do this!"

"What an ice-breaker!" Joanna replied, smiling, "After that experience, I think we're definitely meant to be in this all together. We were quite a team."

"Onwards and upwards," quoted Curtis as we all smiled beginning to relax, already bonded by today's trauma.

Joanna's aspiration was soon proved to be right; the four of us quickly gelled, looking out for one another other without rancour, during the two years to come.

In 1963 qualifying for a career in radiography and achieving Diploma status required two years study with examinations at the end of each course. For some unknown reason, (least never explained to us) part one would involve nineteen months tuition in

Physics, Anatomy and Hospital Practice tested by examinations at Queen's Square, London.

All three subjects needed a pass grade to press on to part two, this time mastering Photography, Radiographic Technique, Radiographic Equipment and an oral examination based on our practical abilities. Part two was scheduled to be held at the same venue seven months after part one. With three difficult subjects to master its timing seemed very strange.

There was also the criterion of a minimum age level, which meant I could not qualify with my compatriots within the two years. Our first set of exams would fall on April 1965, exactly on my nineteenth birthday, the requisite age determined by the Society. However I would be five months too young to take Part Two with the others, in November 1965, so would have to wait until April 1966, to reach the obligatory age of twenty before sitting the qualifying examinations.

Always too young and all very frustrating, but better to get started now than wait another year, so I pushed that problem away and concentrated on achieving all the knowledge necessary to get through Part One. We all had challenges ahead of us, not least becoming capable of understanding radiation physics!

The first four weeks of our training was to take place on the medical and surgical wards spending two weeks on each. We were to be split up and directed to shadow one of the state registered nurses, who would become our mentor and guide. It was her responsibility to see her pupil competent in many basic nursing skills.

There was a formidable list for us to complete, which included: laying a sterile trolley, taking observation readings of temperature, respiration, pulse and blood pressure (no fancy equipment, just a stethoscope and sphygmomanometer with its tight cuff blown up by hand and a good set of ears to hear the changing pulse beat through the stethoscope covered arterial point).

Giving an enema was also listed (one area in which I was already fully competent!) the intricate catheterisation of patients, for us girls both sexes but for Curtis only men; there were no male mid-wives, no mixed sexed wards then and it was still unknown for male nurses to work on female wards. We were also to learn how to put up a drip, along with assisting patients to use bed-pans, commodes and bottles. There was no mention of bed making but after four weeks that expertise was to become one of my top areas of proficiency.

At last I was going to work full-time with real patients, so exciting! But of course there was a "downer." What I hadn't grasped was that our hours of duty had to match our mentors and that meant the unpopular regime of split duties.

A nurses day started at 7.00 am and ended at 8.30 pm with four and a half hours taken off somewhere in between. These of course ran through the whole seven days, weekends were no different; days of the week just blurred into each other.

Night staff came on at 8.00pm and installed themselves in Sister's office for a half hour hand over, called "giving the report." This report enabled each patient to be discussed in turn, highlighting their specific needs and any recent procedures or results, thus all relevant information was dutifully passed on to the next group of carers. The night shift would then repeat the procedure to the day nurses before crawling home to bed.

I was never a "lark" so the prospect of getting up at 6.00 am on a cold, damp late Autumn almost winter morning, grab a piece of toast and cycle to the hospital was a very nasty shock and I hated it.

Chapter 13

My first secondment was to the Men's Medical ward situated upstairs in the main wing of the original Georgian building.

My mentor and teacher was Lucinda (of party going fame) now recently qualified as a staff nurse, wearing her state registered badge with pride and the red belt of authority, coupled with an elaborate silver buckle. She was a tall, elegant figure, her attractive face beautifully made-up, with blonde streaked curls neatly topped by a stiffly starched cap. In addition to being "pleasant to the eye" for the male patients of Men's Medical she was also an excellent nurse. This was the ward I had been attached to for the first two weeks.

In Sister's absence Lucinda took total responsibility for a ward of thirty very sick gentlemen. Many, young and old, would die on this ward from pneumonia, diabetes, heart failure, lung disease and cancer, a difficult environment for such a young person to command.

Alongside the thirty beds, were two isolation rooms where highly infectious patients could be barrier nursed until a vacancy occurred at the Isolation Hospital at the edge of Elmbridge. Tuberculosis was still claiming many victims, who were often eventually diagnosed with the illness (although it had long been raging within them), after contracting the disease probably many months ago. At fourteen I had been fortunate enough to receive the then recently developed BCG, tuberculosis vaccination, administered by the school nurse. However much of the population still failed to receive this protection, and much later in my career a student radiographer fell dangerously ill with TB meningitis, affecting her brain, having been infected taking the chest x-ray of a sufferer. It would be tragic if this devastating wasting illness ever took hold again.

During any of sister's absences from the ward, Lucinda deputised for her, eagerly bearing these responsibilities. In that mode, she determined that I should leave her care well-informed, useful but even more important, not capable of inflicting well-intentioned harm on anyone.

Men's Medical ward received patients between approximately fourteen to eighty years. Typically these men were suffering from heart and breathing difficulties, diabetes and immobility problems. The thirty-bedded ward was always fully occupied; as soon as a bed became vacant a new occupant would be whisked up from admission. There was barely time to strip, disinfect the mattress and re-make the bed, whilst the adjoining locker was thoroughly cleaned and the floor area around freshly scrubbed. All this had to be done as quickly as possible, but the change over also had to meet the imposing standards of Sister's approval.

On my first morning I arrived wearing a freshly laundered white coat nipped in around my waist by such a stiff white belt, so rigid that it rendered any forward bending impossible. Now, as a non-nursing member of staff but a radiographic student, to my utter delight, the silly white cap of my cadetship was no longer required. I was pleased to be five minutes early, feeling quietly confident that my appearance was correct and looking forward to the morning ahead.

Lucinda stopped in front of me, looking critically, whilst she examined my frame up and down. All was clearly not well. She took me to one side and quietly but firmly said, "Barrett, the patients do not need reminding that you have just got out of bed." I flushed, my previous self-satisfied demeanour disappearing rapidly, "Tomorrow," she continued, "you will come wearing enough lipstick and facial colour for them not to offer to change places with you. Truly, you look nearer to death than they do! We are here to care for them and brighten their day a little, not give concern that you are not up to the job. You look as pale as a ghost!"

Well I certainly wasn't expecting that! I had imagined the wearing of cosmetics to be frowned upon, but on reflection I could see she had a point. Lucinda turned around and we entered the ward together. She went to each bed in turn smiling gently, sympathising softly with, "Good morning" to every patient, even the one or two who appeared to be unconscious. That small act of greeting gave patients notice that a different set of nurses had taken over their care.

Lucinda went on to explain to me, " Barrett, always remember that hearing is the last sense to be lost in an unconscious state and the first to be regained, therefore nurses should never, ever, talk over or ignore a seemingly comatosed patient." My learning had already begun.

On the ward that first day was Robert, a young lad of fourteen, struggling to recover from pneumonia, his laboured breathing frequently interspersed by a merciless cough. He was propped semi-upright, his white-faced merging with the pillow. Robert was small for his age, still child-like, as puberty had not yet angled the softness of his body; his upper lip remained free of any fluffy beginnings of a moustache, yet he was deemed too old for the children's ward. To his misfortune he was bedded beside a very frail old man of about eighty years, also suffering from the familiar, raspy breathing of pneumonia. Robert spent his day gazing longingly at the ward clock. He wanted and needed his mum.

Visiting hours were very strict and could be refused or shortened at the discretion of the ward sister. The official timings were 7.00pm – 8.00pm each evening with two visitors only at each bed. An extra hour was allowed on Sunday afternoon between 3.00 and 4.00pm. As soon as the hour hand showed 7.00pm the first person to rush in was Robert's mother, anxiety portrayed by every part of her being. Lucinda told me on occasions a thin, pale man crept in behind her, hating the hospital environment and dreading seeing his son so ill.

He was no use at all, but mum worked her magic, for that one hour at least, as Robert's breathing became quieter and a fleeting, smile momentarily lit his eyes.

To the concern of all, old Tom beside him died in the night. Known colloquially as "old man's friend" pneumonia had taken him off in what was recognised for the very old, a kind departure.

When I arrived the next morning it was to find Robert looking terrified. Even with all the bed curtains drawn he had not been shielded (in that close environment) from the sounds of death and the laying out of Tom's body. He heard the rumble of the body-trolley as it entered the ward to collect the old man, then heard Tom transferred to the body-trolley, next he heard the clunk as its lid was tightly closed and finally, heard the ponderous movements of the night porters as they wheeled Tom's corpse from the ward. The boy knew he was suffering the same illness and now totally believed this also would be his end.

Sister watched Robert's decline that morning with horror, then hurriedly left the ward to consult with Matron. She returned with a purposeful stride. It had been agreed that being exposed so vividly to the sounds of death had been too much for this young man, so for once the rules would be relaxed and two porters soon arrived to transfer him to the children's ward. I was given the task to accompany him as he gripped the sides of the trolley fearful of what lay ahead. As we approached the double doors the young ward sister welcomed him with a lovely smile. He raised his head to see the walls decorated with children's story characters then lay back with a sigh of relief. I handed over all the relevant paperwork and left the nursing staff to settle him in.

Thank goodness it had been obvious to both ward sisters and Matron that Robert had no rampant thoughts about young girls, for despite his teenage years he was still a child himself.

In my break time I popped to the children's ward to see how Robert was getting on. He was seated in a chair beside his bed reading a story to a small boy, his breathing was at last easier and with extended visiting from 5.00pm -7.00pm he would be able to appreciate more loving times with his mum. His fear of death had gone all he wanted was to get well as quickly as he could.

Another useful lesson learnt, medical care wasn't necessarily the whole treatment; although holistic thinking had yet to become an integral part of hospital caring, too many inflexible "Victorian" style rules still controlled nursing. It would take some considerable time, before positively linking recovery to many other aspects of treatment, including the most suitable environment possible.

During my two weeks another teenager was admitted as an emergency. He was Keith, a young man of seventeen, this time, with his dark stubbled chin, definitely beyond the remit of the children's ward. As he arrived I was just finishing the disinfectant cleaning of the locker he was to use, next to the only vacant bed. Two porters wheeled in the trolley transporting this gaunt, unconscious figure hooked up to an intravenous drip. Poking the two long wooden poles down the tubular side recesses of the stretcher cloth, they effortlessly lifted him over onto the awaiting mattressed bed, flanked by two nurses.

There seemed nothing to this new arrival. His lengthy frame made only a slight impression in the draw-sheeted mattress as he lay recumbent and immobile. His drip feed was carefully regulated whilst lightweight covers were drawn over to conceal Keith's underweight torso. I followed Lucinda along with two student nurses to Sister's office where his medical details and treatment plan were to be discussed. We stood in a semi-circle around

Sister's desk eager to find out about Keith's condition. She perched her glasses at the end of her nose, then commanding our respectful attention began to instruct us in an all too common, chronic illness.

"Keith Walter is seventeen years of age. He was admitted in what appears to be a diabetic coma. There are two types of diabetic comas. One, the body has stopped producing insulin from the special cells in the pancreas long enough for too much sugar to be present in the blood stream, even though the kidneys have been excreting it as fast as possible," said sister, then seeing my uncertainty she went on to explain, "Keith would have been passing urine all the time, ("peeing," whispered one of the nurses in my ear, which of course I knew!) As his body tried to get rid of the surplus. After a while ketones are produced, which start to break down good cells and the patient becomes comatose, and without treatment will die. The second diabetic coma is caused by having too much insulin in the blood stream and not sufficient sugar with which to balance the hormone, typically occurring in diagnosed diabetics who have either, not eaten enough or at the correct time or have used up their sugar in excessive exercise or have mistakenly overdosed their insulin injection. It is a complicated condition requiring a disciplined attitude, regular balanced meals and frequent self-monitoring, to achieve the right combination for a normal lifestyle."

I wondered if I could ever remember all of this; and this was only one of the chronic conditions I would need to understand.

"Keith has had no previous symptoms of diabetes," she continued, "so we can conclude that the loss of functioning insulin cells is a recent, though now permanent, event. Once those cells are defunct they will never recover. He will now need daily injections of insulin and a controlled diet. It is our task to get him balanced on the correct dose of insulin, able to do all his own injections and understand how to manage and stick to the correct meals at the correct times, every day. Diabetes is for life!"

I came away from Sister's office feeling upset and in bad humour. "Wow," I thought, once this young man has regained consciousness he will have to understand his life has changed for ever. What a tough time awaited him, just when he could begin to enjoy independence, fun with his mates and possible girlfriends now that he had left school and childhood behind. Perhaps he was planning college or a career of some sorts, it all seemed grossly unfair.

Keith didn't awake for two days, still unaware that his parents spent every minute of visiting time, talking and touching him, trying to get a response as the drip fed his body with the nutrients it so badly craved.

He gradually came to, huge eyes encircled by black shadows as if painted mask-like on to his pale, luminous skin.   Lucinda sat beside him and I hovered, feeling intrusive and gawky behind her.

"Keith, good to see you, now I can get to know you properly and help you to get back to normal; in fact," she said calmly, "you will soon feel much better than you have for months, once we have got your medication and diet sorted out."

She turned to me and directed me off to another task at the other end of the ward. Lucinda knew that explaining what now faced Keith daily and for the rest of his life, injections and monitoring, controlled exercise and a strict carbohydrate diet with all the disastrous consequences if not followed, would devastate him and take all her nursing skills to persuade him that his life still had a future, and more importantly held promise.

Over the next week I watched as doctors explained how his body needed and used insulin, how several nurses helped him with injection technique, practising on an orange and how the dietician came by daily to teach him which foods suited him best, adding up a perfect carbohydrate score for each meal and snack, timed to balance his medication.

Keith was a bright young man expecting to go away to teacher training college as soon as he was eighteen. I dreaded to think how anyone less able coped with these reams of instructions, knowing that another coma, which could result in death, was the price of getting it wrong.

One afternoon when he was feeling really down Lucinda strode over to his bed, "Keith, you have two choices either you sink or you swim! You are a good-looking lad with a bright future so snap out of it and master all you have to learn here, then go home and get on with life!" She immediately turned and strode off without waiting for a response, sometimes tough love worked, it was tough on her too I realised spotting her flushed cheeks and eyes shining with emotion.

I finished my secondment to Men's Medical on the day Keith's parents came to fetch him home. They presented the nurses with a large box of chocolates in gratitude, something their son would no longer be able to indulge in. We all knew they also had to learn a whole new way of life to help keep Keith well. I have often wondered if it worked out for them all, hoping he had been able to follow his dreams and live his "normal" life.

After my two weeks shadowing Lucinda I was passed over to the Women's Surgical Ward to work and learn under the supervision of Maureen. She was a senior staff-nurse having qualified five years previously and was hopefully awaiting a Sister's post to become vacant.

It was a busy, bustling, rather noisy ward with patients constantly leaving and returning from their operations, trundled out and back on theatre trolleys. There were three operating theatres with a very small recovery unit so mostly patients returned quickly from theatre. Back on the ward a nurse was allocated to "special" them by constantly taking observation readings throughout the difficult post operation period, tying up one member of the team for several hours as these carefully recorded observations could reveal internal bleeding, perforated intestines leading to peritonitis following surgery or breathing problems resulting from anaesthesia.

Elmbridge was in the planning stage for a much needed Intensive Care Unit (ICU) to be added to the theatre suite. Following the success of the Special Care Baby Unit down the road at the maternity hospital, the management committee realised that specialist equipment and nursing care would give patients the best chance of recovery immediately after surgery in a dedicated area, manned by theatre staff including anaesthetists. It would also release nurses on the ward from the responsibility and time-consuming post-operative observation role.

These plans costing vast amounts of money, would not find funding magically appearing from government resources, instead most likely was a hefty input from the local Hospital League of Friends. This association, which included a well respected group of prominent business men, organized fund raising activities all year round; dances, dinners, summer fetes, Xmas bazaars, raffles and the like. These events took place every year to accrue quite large sums of money, purely for the use of the general hospital.

Whilst I was attached to Women's Surgical, Martin made frequent visits to the ward. To my horror he was going out with Jane the ward sister and would make any excuse to call in, not only to see her but to spy on me, checking I was learning as much as possible. With that in mind Maureen spared me nothing.

I gave suppositories, laid up sterile trolleys and even learnt how to put up a drip. One of my least favourite tasks was to assist with a flatulence tube insertion. When a patient became bloated with painful abdominal gas a rubber hose-like tube was pushed into their rectum, then very quickly (speed here was essential for the well-being of the rest of the ward) the outlet end was immersed in a bucket of water, where volumes of vigorous bubbles rushed to the surface bringing a relieved smile to the patient's face. Too late with the immersion in water then the faecal smell appeared to linger for days!

At last, our first month was completed and because of the constant attention to all shapes and sizes of human body parts I was conquering that demeaning tell-tale rush of blood to my face. Just for that it had been worth it.

Now we four students had finished working so closely with the nurses, they took an interest in our progress, friendships had been forged and a greater understanding of what went on in the x-ray department began to develop.

It was now late November and the raw coldness that had greeted the early morning cycle rides had been my only negative experience throughout that month; still I had to concede I was quite relieved they were over.

Chapter 14

Monday morning saw us back in the department, pleased to be together once more swapping our nursing experiences, the more bizarre and extreme the better. Now our professional training began in earnest as every Wednesday we were to set off for our academic tuition at Brunswick General Hospital.

Linda and I caught the train and Joanne just continued her rail journey by a further three stations. Curtis, wrapped up in a huge tan, suede, sheepskin jacket and sporting a white crash helmet and massive leather gloves putt putted his way on a Lambretta scooter, its "L plate" dangling from the rear number plate. He arrived bitterly cold with a purple nose and glowing cheeks to meet up with us at Brunswick School for Nurses.

We found our way to the small classroom reserved for our lectures, which was equipped with a black board, roll down screen and slide projector and two rows of wooden desks accompanied by hard seated and straight-backed chairs; little chance of nodding off in such austere surroundings.

We filed into the room, where six unknown girls stood "en-masse" filling the space with lively chatter.

"Oh! Hello," said a tall brown haired student, "You must be the Elmbridge bunch. I'm Susan and this is Barbara, Janet, Jennifer, Monica and Sandra," introducing each in turn. "We've got name labels to put on to help everyone know who's who, perhaps you better do the same, except I don't think anyone will confuse you!" she added nodding at Curtis as she handed labels and a pen to him.

"Well, even so it will help the lecturers," he replied stiffly, turning about to introduce each of us.

There was a nervous, edgy feel of anticipation about all of us, rather like the start of a new school year and already we four sensed an atmosphere of "them and us." They were pleasant enough but seemed to regard us as poor cousins, quickly voiced by Jennifer. "I applied to Elmbridge School too," she offered with a knowing smile, "but found it too parochial. I felt the smallness of your x-ray department would limit my learning experience so I decide Brunswick would be a much better option and came here."

"And for that we will be eternally grateful," beamed back Curtis. It seemed the battle lines had already been drawn.

Thankfully before their conversation could degenerate further, Miss South, Superintendent Radiographer strode in. "Good morning everyone, now please be seated, while we make our introductions."

This formidable lady managed an eight-roomed x-ray department, with fifteen qualified staff, working along side four consultant radiologists. She was also the lead tutor and organiser of this radiographic school and served on the National Board of the Society of Radiographers; at examination time she set and marked papers. Her enthusiasm for her work was boundless.

Miss South was a dumpy, middle-aged lady of about forty two, with a "gung-ho" voice and manner, which reminded me of my old hockey mistress at school. She had a great sense of humour but could swiftly become very severe if crossed. She was a confirmed spinster, sharing her home with another professional lady. They both, she described, had lost the love of their lives in the war and thus supported each other. But in the 1960's same sex relationships were taboo so that any revelation that instead they were a loving couple would have stopped both their careers in their tracks, hence her need to explain her living situation to a group of students.

The stigma of lesbianism was total, it was never spoken of and I in all innocence completely accepted what she said and never queried why she had needed to give us details of her private life. Later that day Curtis laughed at my naivety as he proceeded to enlighten me about male and female homosexuality. It seems amazing today, that aged seventeen I sat open mouthed, blushing furiously while he set the facts before me.

Miss South was a bouncy, energetic person void of make-up with a glowing complexion, which belied her indoor occupation within a department lacking any natural light. She made her lectures both informative and fun and on this first day of formal tuition, she delivered a lively lecture full of funny anecdotes to launch us into the subject of Hospital Practice. By the time her hour was completed we were all more relaxed with one another but that was not to last.

"Ladies and gentleman, I need to inform you of the itinerary for next Wednesday. I will meet you at the front entrance to the hospital, then, escort you to the mortuary, which is unmarked at the rear of the hospital. I will leave you in the care of Dr. Schwann the Consultant Pathologist. He will lecture you whilst performing a post-mortem on a cadaver. At this early stage in your studies you need to see the reality of the main organs, their size, shape, relation to each other and position in the body. X-ray details only in two dimensions, you need to understand the body's internal structure in all three. This lecture is a compulsory part of our training here at Brunswick and I know you will find the morning very worthwhile."

She gathered up her papers, beamed, "Good-bye," leaving us standing, somewhat stunned, at her rapid departure, which gave no opportunity for questions regarding her announcement.

A general burble of anxious chatter erupted, so that we hardly noticed our next lecturer quietly enter the room. His smothered cough brought us to attention; this was to be the first anatomy lecture, which I had been awaiting with interest.

The lecturer was one of the consultant radiologists, a tall grey haired, pale-faced man wearing an ill-fitting and slightly dishevelled grey suit, arriving ten minutes late.

"I'm sorry to be a few minutes late; for those who are new here I am Dr. Forsyth, shall we make a start."

He spoke very quietly, mumbling reminders to himself, then produced Grey's Anatomy (the anatomical bible at the time) from a battered briefcase. He opened this wonderful encyclopaedia of the human body and proceeded to read from page 1, in a rather stilted manner. He gave subsequent explanations by illustrating with an accompanying diagram on the blackboard, drawn little bigger than a postcard. As his voice became more and more hypnotic it was very hard to stay awake, even on these chairs. Fortunately I had picked up quite a lot of anatomical terminology and jargon during my cadetship but much of this first lecture seemed a foreign language to the others.

We broke for lunch and the four of us hurried off, away from the others, to a nearby pub "The Fox and Hound," anxious to discuss the planned post-mortem and our opinions of the Brunswick students. Hastily, we downed our half-pint glasses of lager and lime and steeled ourselves for that one lecture we were all dreading, Physics.

On our return, the Physics lecturer was already writing on the blackboard while we took our seats. He was Dr. Stringer, who led the Hospital's team of physicists based in the Radiotherapy department, where treatment plans for using radiation to kill off cancer cells were formulated by these scientists and their technicians. Sadly this early balding, bespectacled, learned gentleman, drowning in a white coat three times too big for him, was incapable of dropping to our basic level of knowledge and took us on a journey of atoms, electrons and energy where he lost me completely, not a good beginning.

We left the confines of the classroom about 4.00pm rushing to the station to grab a brick hard bread roll, filled with rubbery cheese, and a lukewarm coffee from the British Rail smoke filled café, before travelling home.

During the next week none of us mentioned the forthcoming post mortem, perhaps by not speaking about it we hoped it would go away, but of course next Wednesday arrived all too quickly. I had never seen a dead body and with the all too recent, painful recollections of my previous panicky reactions in casualty, when confronted by a dislodged eyeball or mangled stumps of fingers, I was in dread of the morning's planned performance. I knew there was no hiding from it, "Compulsory!" Miss South had insisted, so I filled my pockets with packets of Polo mints and met up with Linda at the station on this cold, bright winter's day.

She was bubbling with enthusiasm, "Hello, Mary, how are you?" she asked, not waiting for an answer, "I'm so looking forward to this morning, aren't you? It should be very helpful to see everything as it really is, position and size especially!"

"Yes, well, hope so…" I managed lamely.

"Hey, you're not happy about it are you? Come on don't worry, you were great with that lawn mower man's fingers bleeding all over you, and this time there will be no heart pumping fresh blood around, so no big deal."

I gave a weak smile and changed the subject to Dr. Stringer's fearsome physics lecture, and then we happily derided the Brunswick girls for the rest of the journey.

We met up with Curtis and Joanna looking calm and relaxed, well wrapped up against the morning chill. They were standing a little way apart from the Brunswick students, when Miss South marched briskly towards everyone. With a swift greeting she turned to check our attendance into her register, then led us around the back path to the unmarked mortuary. Double, plain wooden doors stood open to receive us into a large white-tiled surgical arena, with bright fluorescent lighting reflecting from every surface. The inside temperature was not much greater than that of outside, so we kept our coats on, just removing scarves and gloves. I stuffed my hands in my pockets to be comforted by a packet of Polo's. There were two "butler" sinks, two metallic surfaced examination tables, surrounded by a grey tiled floor interrupted by several large drainage grates. Two long hoses were attached and coiled, like huge red snakes, around wall-mounted taps. Several steel buckets stood at the edge of the room and a strong metal arm swung out, supporting three long red rubber aprons. X-ray viewing boxes gleamed their bright lights making the whole scene whiter than white.

There were scales, receivers, instruments and all manner of equipment positioned for ease of access, for the pathologist whilst working on a cadaver (corpse). A large, white-coated doctor stood waiting while we spaced ourselves around him. He signalled to his assistant to close the doors behind us.

"Good morning. I am Doctor Schwann." He addressed us in a heavy guttural accent, making these few words sound more like an order than a greeting.

"Good morning," we dutifully replied.

"You will stand here at the pathology table so," he indicated to us to take up a semi-circle around the table's working surface. "I shall move around and explain while I work. If you have any questions, that is good, I can stop and respond at any time, the patient won't die," he paused chuckling, "for he is already dead!"

Goodness if that's his attempt at being funny, how will I survive this? I asked myself, unwanted panic beginning to creep into my mind.

"Dominic, fetch our first cadaver," he instructed, turning to put great white boots on his feet and hoisting a large red apron over his head. Next he pulled on thin plastic gloves and took a sharp scalpel between his thumb and index finger.

Dominic returned with assistance, then, these two orderlies transferred a covered human form onto the table, carefully removing the sheeting to reveal a young adult male. Truthfully there was nothing to fear.

His body appeared to me akin to an empty box, rather like finding a vacated crab or whelk shell, its contents missing. There was light stubble on his chin, fair straggly hair creeping over his ears and a waxen, creamy texture to his skin but this unique person had gone.

"The young man lying here collapsed suddenly, playing at the football for his town. He arrived here at the hospital, dead, so now we find out why, that is my job, look for clues, look for causes, there was a reason, I will find it!" he concluded quite dramatically, then paused, looking up at us all as he poised to make his first incision. But before he could proceed, Jennifer began an urgent fit of coughing, then turned about and dived, retching over the nearest sink, where she fast deposited her earlier breakfast. Dr. Schwann raised his caterpillar eyebrows at Dominic, who escorted the shaking student from the room. Clearly this was such a common occurrence it merited no comment.

Once again he turned to the corpse and this time successfully exposed the contents of the thorax. Sucking hard on my Polo mint, I began to really listen and study all that had been revealed and to my surprise become completely absorbed in the whole morning's proceedings. Miss South had been right, it was a necessary lesson, bringing Grey's Anatomical diagrams into reality, far beyond anything Dr. Forsyth would achieve. That morning left us in wonderment at the construction of the human body. We were excited by all we had seen.

Jennifer failed to reappear in the afternoon and was again missing the following week.

It appeared that both Jennifer and Miss South had decided that she was not suited to a medical career, instead changing to a teacher training course might be a better option. Miss South's lady companion was on the board of the Brunswick teacher training college, and to everyone's relief managed to secure a late entry position for Jennifer.

Back at Elmbridge our tutorial sessions with Mr. Petrie had begun. He was now the Superintendent Radiographer, following Sister Aster's retirement but much to our sorrow had retained his teaching role. He was a shy, awkward little man, technically brilliant and carried out all the major complex examinations with ease, but his charisma and ability to communicate facts clearly were non-existent.

We came to dread his tutorials at the radiographer's sitting room, which he had decide to resume now he held the position of superintendent radiographer and therefore more able to deal with the displeasure of Home Sister. We felt that armed with

Elizabeth's first year notes and reams of books, we could manage far better without him.

To catch up with Elizabeth at this point, she had started her second year having passed her Part 1 examinations successfully; the other target she had set herself had also been achieved following her engagement to the charming and good-looking, Indian registrar, Sayeed Ahmed.

One evening they invited me to dinner at his lodgings in the next street to the hospital. She of course still lived in the Nurses' Home, cohabitation before marriage would have ended her studies as Home Sister would have certainly found out and that would have been the end of Elizabeth's career.

Young couples were expected to only consummate their relationships after marriage. Sex before this union and heaven forbid pregnancy, were considered shocking, costing many single, expectant women to be shunned at home and at work.

There was a large house at the outskirts of the town called "The House of the Good Shepherd" where such girls as Betty, whose early x-ray had confirmed her pregnancy, were cared for up until delivery, and for a short while after, by nuns. There, the solution for most was for their baby to be matched for adoption with a couple desperate but unable to start their own family. Very few of these girls were able to go it alone or have family support once the baby was born.

It was the fear of most middle-aged parents that their unmarried daughters would become an "unmarried mother" stigmatised by gossiping neighbours and relatives. It took the freedom of the "pill," over many years, to relax society's scorn towards these young women, whilst they often never recovered from having to part with their child. However, although Elizabeth resided at the Nurses' Home, she and Sayeed had the sanctuary of his rented house, and how they spent their time within it was their business, far from gossips and prying eyes.

I was so pleased to see how happy Elizabeth looked as she prepared Spaghetti Bolognese for our supper. I had neither seen nor tasted this dish, although my mother was a good cook only English food was set upon our table. I watched intrigued as Elizabeth fed stiff, brittle sticks like thin, yellow straws into a saucepan of boiling water. The resulting puffed up, light cream intertwined tubes posed the question, and how did you eat this?

The sauce looked similar to the base of Mum's cottage pie, which I loved so in spite of eating messily (which was tactfully ignored), I enjoyed my first pasta supper.

We spent a lovely evening together, Elizabeth had always treated me as an equal and in her company my shyness disappeared. Sayeed told me that once she had achieved her radiographic qualification in April, he was going to apply for a G.P. post in the West Country. From this I gathered that the supper was really an early good-bye meal for us to share. I knew how much I would miss her support; she had given me such strength and friendship when I was being hounded as the most junior being in the department.

Elizabeth went on to gain a good pass mark in all her Part 2 examinations, kindly leaving all her notes and books for the four of us to study. She alone knew how tough the academic side of our course had been because of the poor quality lectures, but hopefully following her example, we agreed, that if she could make it through alone, by helping each other we should make it too.

Chapter 15

Stella and David Garnish had been married for four years, she was twenty-seven and he was two years older. For the past eighteen months they had been trying to start a family. It was time, they both thought, to become parents.

From the first month of ceasing contraception, Stella expected to be pregnant; after all, while they were courting her mother had continuously warned her that any "hanky panky" before marriage would immediately lead to a baby.

As each month passed she began to fret; what was the matter? Were they doing "it" wrong? Why didn't she fall for a baby like her best friend Joy? It was all a puzzle. David had been less concerned and tried to reassure her, but after a year and a half they decided something must be wrong and plucked up courage to see their G.P., Dr. Jameson.

"It's probably nothing, only nature taking its time, "he offered smiling. "But I'm afraid I can't start investigations until you have been trying unsuccessfully for two years, so if nothing happens in the next six months come back and see me and then we will start looking for an answer."

Month after month disappointment followed disappointment.

Stella treated herself to little gifts, a new pair of gloves or a pretty necklace, telling herself, "All the time I'm working I'm pretty lucky because now I can afford to spend money on myself."

But she knew it was a lie. Why were there so many pregnant women in town lately and couples pushing prams? Every time she went to town, they seemed to be waiting for her to get off the bus, taunting her. David and Stella became regimented in their love making, aiming to match the rise in temperature on her thermometer, passion and joy being replaced by the urgency to catch the fleeting days of ovulation.

The six months dragged by until once again they sat before Dr. Jameson. He studied the tenseness between them; the added worry lines on this young woman's face, and felt how fragile their marriage had become.

He chose his words carefully knowing they would hang on to every syllable.

Right now, Mr. and Mrs. Garnish, we will get to work to find out all about this *temporary* infertility. First a few tests for you, Mr. Garnish, to check your sperm count and find out if the sperm we find are capable of reaching the right place. We can do those while we wait for an appointment for you both to attend Mr. Beamish, Consultant Gynaecologist, in his Infertility Clinic at Elmbridge Hospital. That way we aren't wasting any more time. My best advice meanwhile is to try and relax a little, it isn't always possible to conceive but it is more likely to happen when making love is more than making a baby!"

Stella glanced guiltily at David knowing that this is just what was happening to her, and resolved to try and recover the closeness that had existed between them a year ago. Thank goodness they were at last on the road to finding the cause of their problem and hopefully putting it right. Maybe, knowing that would help her to relax more as Dr. Jameson had advised.

David's pathology result was returned, at the same time as their hospital appointment card dropped through the letterbox. It was a positive finding, with a satisfactory amount of vigorous sperm in his sample. To their relief the Infertility Clinic date was set, only two more weeks to wait.

David and Stella sat alongside three other couples outside Mr. Breamish's clinic door. Nervous half smiles were exchanged as each pair recognised the anxious anticipation they all felt.

"Mr. and Mrs. Garnish please!" called out the clinic nurse batting their case folder in the air. David gripped Stella's hand tightly in his own as they followed her through the door, closing it firmly behind them.

"Good morning, Mr. and Mrs. Garnish. Please sit there, Mr. Garnish while I take your wife behind the screen for a 'quick look see'," instructed this large, fresh-faced doctor as he straightway whisked Stella out of sight.

With eighteen couples booked for the morning clinic he had little time to waste on pleasantries, but tried hard to relate to each pair hoping to put his patients at ease. Subjecting these young people to discuss the most intimate aspect of their relationships was a delicate task; he had to gain their trust.

"Fine, good, slip your things back on and join us when you are ready." David heard him say, as Mr. Beamish returned to his desk and began to fill out a series of forms.

Stella joined them and sat down beside her husband grasping his hand in hers.

"Well very good so far, no obvious physical problems with you Mrs. Garnish, and Dr. Jameson's results for you," he added nodding at David, "were also good, so we must press on and try and identify the cause of this infertility. Mrs. Garnish the next step is for you to have a special x-ray known, as an HSG, which will show up your uterus and fallopian tubes (the egg carrying passages.) If one or both of these tubes are blocked or your uterus is unusual in any way, this investigation will tell us what is wrong. I will be there to perform the procedure with radiographers taking these clever pictures. Now, take this form down to x-ray and book your appointment for as soon as possible. It will have to fit in with your monthly cycle but hopefully you won't have to wait very long."

He stood up in dismissal and shook their hands.

"Nurse, send me in the next couple please," he instructed as the door closed behind them.

The equipment in Room 3 was set up, the trolley was laid with the special, sterile, HSG pack containing Mr. Beamish's required gynaecological instruments, also syringes and underneath the ampoules of iodine based, contrast fluid, "the dye."

Jeanette, the senior radiographer, was to be in charge of the x-ray procedure for Mrs. Garnish's examination.

David and Stella were sitting, holding hands in a tight clasp as they waited anxiously in the narrow department corridor.

Jeanette approached them, "Hello there Mrs. Garnish, can you come and get changed now?" she asked. "There are three female student radiographers currently studying this x-ray examination, do you have any objection to them being present for your investigation?" "No, no of course not if it helps them to learn, I just want to get it over with and find out what's wrong," she replied, taking the proffered white gown.

"Thank you," smiled Jeanette, "Stay where you are when you've changed, I will come and fetch you when Mr. Beamish arrives."

She returned to Room 3, "Linda, Joanna and Mary you can all stay and watch but please be discrete with your presence, this is an intimate investigation and the patient's sensibilities must be considered throughout."

We all nodded, delighted that we would be able to watch and learn. Just at that moment Mr. Beamish walked in, greeting us all as he marched to the sink to scrub his hands, before pulling on sterile gloves and carefully opening his pack out, checking that everything he needed was included. At his nod of approval Jeanette left to fetch his patient.

Mr. Beamish approached his patient saying, "Hello, Mrs. Garnish, let me explain exactly what is going to happen. I shall very gently insert, a hollow cannula into your cervix, the opening to your womb, then fill it with this fluid," he pointed to one of the ampoules on the trolley. "By pushing the fluid in with the syringe, there will be enough pressure to cause it to spill over into your egg carrying tubes, which will show us if they are blocked in any way, thereby stopping your eggs getting through. Do you understand or have any questions?" he asked.

"Well only that the fluid looks clear, so how does it show up if I can see right through it?" "You might be able, to but x-rays can't! It will make your fallopian tubes and your uterus look white on the films. Sometimes, mind only sometimes, if there is a small blockage, pushing this fluid through can clear it."

Satisfied that Stella had understood all that he had told, he asked her to climb up onto the x-ray table for the insertion of the cannula, which he proceeded to do with expert ease. Bearing in mind Jeanette's instructions, we three students had disappeared behind the protective screen of the control panel, until our patient had been turned onto her back and her modesty regained, but with the cannula in place. Jeanette positioned both the film under and x-ray camera exactly over Stella's pelvis and gave her the breathing instructions. Joanna helped Mr. Beamish don a protective, double sided, lead rubber apron, for he was to stay "in the field" during the x-ray exposure.

"OK, are you ready girls?" he called, while Jeanette joined us at the control panel and set the correct exposure.

"Yes!" she replied.

"Injecting now, take your picture!" he commanded, pushing hard on the plunger of the filled syringe.

"Hold your breath keep very still Mrs. Garnish," called out Jeanette, pressing the exposure button and the familiar clunk, click sound matched the meter needle swinging across its dial, recording a positive exposure.

Linda took the film from its tray and rushed off to Stuart in the darkroom. All the instruments were to stay in place in case another film was needed so Jeanette stood quietly chatting to Mrs. Garnish, reassuring her that everything was going as planned, while Mr. Beamish stood to one side carefully keeping his gloved hands, out of range of any non-sterile surfaces.

Linda returned, placing the dripping film in front of the room's lit viewing box. Mr. Beamish stood in close, peering, then stepped back still scrutinising the black and white image.

He turned to Mrs. Garnish, "Well my dear, the right tube is patent, shown here clearly, which is great news. The left appears to have a small kink in it so I am going to push one more syringe full of fluid through, hoping the force will straighten that little bend out," he announced cheerfully. The procedure was repeated and once again we waited, this time for the second film.

Linda quickly returned and positioned the new film on the viewing box.

"Good, good!" he cried, delightedly. "Look the kink has nearly gone." He grabbed the film and waved in front of the recumbent lady, pointing out the detail, for her to see and believe. "My dear you have two good tubes, all ready to carry your eggs to a normal uterus. Go home and with your husband, get busy, let nature take its course."

He removed the instruments and peeled off his gloves. "Make an appointment for my clinic in three months time before you leave. Goodbye my dear," he said walking out to the corridor, where I watched him stop to quietly impart the good news to Mr. Garnish. No wonder his patients trusted him, not only was he an excellent doctor but also a perfect gentleman.

Stella quickly changed and rushed out to David. He hugged her tightly as they both thanked Jeanette. It truly was an emotive procedure, but Jeanette's calm, professional demeanour throughout the afternoon was a positive lesson to all three of us.

About ten months later a heavily pregnant woman walked slowly down the long corridor supported by an attentive husband. By chance Jeanette was working in the general room and picked up a request form for a pregnancy x-ray.

She glanced at the patient's name and a huge grin spread across her face. "Mary, Linda, Joanna," she called, knowing we were having a quick cuppa in the tearoom. We all emerged quickly, wondering what was up. "Look at the name, you surely remember Mrs. Garnish, the first HSG you all saw, well here she is with an x-ray request querying twins!" She hurried off anxious to catch up with her patient and share her excitement. The three of us rushed round to the wet viewing room to await Jeanette's film and sure enough, within minutes, she was able to point out to us two babies lying curled round head to toe. Word soon spread round the whole department bringing smiles all around. Sometimes, just sometimes, one of our investigative procedures achieves a very happy ending

After their long, sometimes painful wait, Stella and David were now to be parents to an instant family. Those two frustrating and anxious years faded quickly from their minds as they prepared for the two babies to be born. David worked busily each evening, clearing out their second dingy bedroom, which had long been used to store bits and pieces and converting it into a cheerful nursery. They decided on primrose yellow walls with lilac curtains, as they had no idea what sex the twins were, then purchased two white cots with colourful animal transfers inside and out.

Stella often stroked her huge bump in wonderment hardly daring to believe their dream had come true, but sudden healthy kicking soon proved that her impending motherhood was very real indeed. Two weeks after Stella had attended for her pregnancy x-ray, Jeanette found a letter waiting for her on the department reception desk. She pulled from the envelope an embossed card announcing the safe arrival of Samuel and Sarah Garnish, which she turned over and with moist eyes read:

"We have been blessed with two beautiful babies. There aren't words enough to say how grateful we are to you and Mr. Beamish, for we have no doubt that your special x-ray worked its miracle for us. Stella and David x

Chapter 16

At the end of a particularly tedious anatomy lecture given by Dr. Forsyth, Miss South came striding in.

"Before you all disappear for lunch, I need to tell you about a forthcoming change to you training routine. You will be attending both Hammersmith Hospital and Maida Vale Neurological Hospital, in London, for tuition in areas we cannot cover here in Brunswick. A compulsory part of your curriculum is to have experienced and understood, specialised techniques to examine the heart and circulatory systems as well as the brain and nervous system, all of which has to be logged and counter signed in your practical book. You will attend these sessions in pairs, spending two weeks in each in order to get the most benefit from the visits. I shall be arranging accommodation at the nearest Youth Hostels and confirm the details with you next week. The Brunswick students will go first, starting Monday week; four weeks later it will be your turn Elmbridge. Is that clear?"

"There are five of us now," piped up Janet.

Miss South sighed and gave her a withering look, "Obviously, there will be three in one group, Janet, and two in the other," she replied scathingly. "Anything else?"

"Yes Miss South," Joanna stood up, looking hard at her, "Thank you, but we at Elmbridge will not require youth hostel lodgings instead, we will be arranging our own accommodation with Mr. Petrie's approval."

Miss South appeared horrified by such interference with her plans, the audacity of our group from Elmbridge had taken her by surprise, but could see that arguing the matter would be undignified, so tossing her head in annoyance she replied, "If that is what you want fine, but your parents must understand that I relinquish responsibility for your well being during that month in London"

"Oh don't worry about us, "replied Joanna, "Mary and I are Londoners and Curtis and Linda are more than capable of managing, so we shall have no problems."

Annoyed by such boldness from Joanna, Miss South gave the four of us a long, cold stare, then turned away and marched from the classroom. Few people defied her and survived, she did not intend for this to go unreported and immediately set off to telephone her displeasure to Mr. Petrie, expecting him to support her by issuing some form of discipline on his arrogant students.

"Well done you!" Curtis patted Joanna on the shoulder, whilst Linda and I beamed in triumph at our escape from Miss South's control. Joanna, grinned, pleased that we supported her brave stand.

"I didn't want us to be separated with Curtis in the YMCA; instead we can book a B&B somewhere between the two hospitals and enjoy the London night life without a curfew." As we suspected, instead of bearing with Miss South, Mr. Petrie was delighted that we had chosen his approval and rebuked her jurisdiction.

"Joanna as you are living in the suburbs just let me see addresses of two establishments that have your parent's approval before you make any bookings. I'll leave it with you then," he added, walking away with a rare, confident smile and straight back, lifted by the knowledge that we students had trusted his judgement above Miss South's.

"No," he decided, "I shan't return her call, she'll just have to accept that my students are mature and independent young people, quite capable of making their own decisions."

We arrived at 33 Artesian Avenue, which was a tall Victorian terraced building, based in Paddington and climbed the six steps to the front door.

A small, slightly harassed looking lady answered our knock. "Hello, I'm Mrs. Eames, you must be the four students, I'm expecting."

"Yes!" We replied in unison.

"Come in, come in," she ushered us through the door. "Right, here is your key girls, you have room 406, and you, young man have room 403. Fourth floor and there's no lift I'm afraid, it's a bit dingy up there, not how I would have it," she added apologetically. Then seeing our puzzled expressions she continued, "Oh! I don't own this place, it's my sister's and she is in Australia visiting her son. He went on one of those £10 emigration ships a while ago. I'm just looking after it for three months while she's gone. I'll do my best by you that's all I can say."

And with that she disappeared into the depths of the Guest House.

We dragged our cases up four flights of stairs, carpeted in crimson and brown, although the design could have been coffee and soup stains. The thick air glistened with tobacco smoke and dust, whenever a thin beam of sunlight penetrated the grimy landing windows but we didn't care. We were free of any adult supervision for four working weeks, so the dingy décor and rock hard beds could not dampen our high spirits. We girls shared a room with one double bed and one single divan, which we decided we would take turns to use, drawing lots to establish who the first lucky occupant would be. Linda won and happily plonked her case at the foot of the single bed, while Joanna and I decided who would sleep nearest the window, which looked over the back yard and its rubbish bins.

"I hope you don't kick!" announced Joanna with a fierce look folding her arms across her chest."

"No, but I snore like a warthog!" I retorted grinning, then seeing her horrified expression, added quickly, "Sorry, only joking silly! I often share a bed with James' girlfriend and she hasn't reported any fearsome habits."

Joanna smiled weakly and apologised, "I have never shared a bed with anyone before. I didn't mean to get so paranoid."

By this time Linda was sitting on her bed already unpacked, "There's not much room in this awful narrow wardrobe, I hope I've left you two enough space."

The tall brown wooden cupboard stood lopsidedly beside a spotted green rug on the otherwise bare yellow linoleum covered floor. Hardly high quality interior design! Above us, almost matching the tone of the floor, spread a tobacco, stained ceiling, which had long turned its shade of murky mustard, while every fibre of bedding and curtains reeked of cheap cigarettes.

Along the corridor, Curtis' tiny single room was next to the shared toilet; at least that facility was separated from the bathroom.

"If I turn over too far in the excitement of my dreams I will get wedged between the bed frame and the wall," he complained, "so if you hear me yelling in the night you will have to come and rescue me! And girls, no flushing that loo in the night else I'll get no sleep," he ordered.

"Don't be daft, you'll sleep through anything after a few lager and limes," laughed Linda. "Speaking of which, time to explore the nearest pub. Come on all of you!" she insisted as we all bundled quickly down the stairs.

Luckily we didn't have to go far, for "The Cat & Fiddle" stood nearby on the corner of our road and it looked a promising cheap evening retreat. It was pretty dark inside with brown painted walls, their dusty plaster swirls skimming over the surface. The surrounding red, mock-leather sofas and chairs were scuffed and any small tears were held together with tape. We squashed together in a bowed corner seat, beside the window, until a lanky barman appeared silently behind the bar and stood expectantly at the pumps waiting for our order.

"We're lodging nearby just up the road," Curtis told the man as he walked over to the bar, "probably make this our local for a few weeks. Four lager and limes, halves please." The bar man gave Curtis a long hard look, "Shan't make much profit from you then," was his curt reply.

"Well we can always go somewhere else!" Curtis retorted sharply, somewhat stung by this reception.

"Ok, Ok, keep your 'air on! *Sir,* I'm sure, you are very welcome," he added with a half-hearted grin, "anyway anyfin's better than nuffin'. Four half-pint lager and limes, coming up."

The Hospital management Committee had allowed us £1.00 per day in expenses. Our Bed & Breakfast took up 15/- of that so after 6d for bus fares we were left with only 4/6d to spend on food. It meant that for the first time in my life I would eat an enormous breakfast, when all I could usually consume was a slice of toast! A cheese roll would suffice for lunch, leaving enough for a lager and lime and a bag of chips in the evening; high living indeed. What did it matter, we were away from parental eyes and control.

We slowly savoured our drinks making them last an hour, then set off to devour freshly fried chips, from the "chippie" next door. He doused them in salt and vinegar, then wrapped them tightly in yesterday's newspaper, its famous faces becoming greasier by the moment. They tasted heavenly. In fact, everything felt great; I was back in the London I had sorely missed.

There was one other guest at breakfast who jumped up immediately we walked into the dining room. He was quite tall and vaguely good-looking in a sort of 'David Niven' debonair film star's manner, with dark, slightly curly hair and a trimmed moustache.

He put his hand out to shake with each of us in turn, "My name is Jim, you must be the students Mrs. Eames mentioned. I'm a sales rep. for 'Delicio' chocolates, I'm sure you've heard of them. We sell at the posh shops, Fortnum and Mason, Harrods and the like." "Pleased to meet you," stepped in Joanna. "This is Curtis, Linda and Mary, I'm Joanna. We're here for four weeks visiting local hospitals." Formalities over Jim, the sales rep returned to his seat and retreated behind his Daily Express newspaper as he did every morning of our stay.

Breakfast was a triumph of sorts. A small tumbler of over sweetened, diluted orange juice with a bowl of cornflakes soaked in watered down milk, heaped with sugar began the feast. This was followed by one sausage, one fried egg, one rasher of bacon half a soggy tomato and ten baked beans, a platter that never varied all week, even to the number of baked beans. We all ate greedily, finishing off with toast, marmalade and two cups of dark brown sweet tea.

As we finished our meal, Curtis produced a shiny penny from his trouser pocket and placed it on the back of his hand ready to decide companions and destinations by the toss of the coin.

"Here we go girls, Linda you call first to see who goes with whom."

She chose heads and won, "I'll go with you Curtis," she decided grinning at us, "have a break from female company, not used to it all day and all night!"

He laughed, seemingly pleased with Linda as his companion.

"Now Joanna you call to choose hospitals." This time Joanna won and picked The Hammersmith Hospital for her and my first two weeks.

It was 8.30 am as we all dashed upstairs to grab our bags, then feeling rather apprehensive hugged and wished each other 'Good luck' before setting off to our different locations.

Chapter 17

The Hammersmith Hospital stood enormously before us as we gazed at it with awe. Joanna stopped a friendly looking porter to beg for assistance.

"That's alright ducks," he grinned. "You both follow Fred, never lost me way yet," his perky, cheerful cockney tones eased my anxious mood as I remembered the resilient London spirit. We twisted and turned down endless corridors until it seemed we could go no lower, here finally was the x-ray department.

"Enjoy yerselves gals, give me a wave next time yer my way," and off he strode with our thanks, another good turn done.

The receptionist directed us to a small office, where a large, buxom Senior Radiographer greeted us. She seemed pleasant enough, but we could tell too many useless students had walked this way, and was happy to dispatch us to the Cardiology Department for our tuition in radiography of the heart. We were issued with white coats and name badges, then, when suitably attired, we dropped the familiar weighty, lead rubber aprons over our heads. Here the staff were very used to visiting students, be they doctors, nurses or radiographers, this was after all a hub of learning into recently perfected techniques, exploring the anatomy of the heart and its great vessels, circulating with 'dye' stained blood around the body. In a series of lit rooms, television monitors replaced the old, dimly glowing, fluorescent screens of my cadetship, which then we had peered at in the dark; here instead, images were boosted many, many times to appear brightly and clearly in front of us. That familiar feeling of magical wonderment struck me once more, how amazing it was going to be to see such detail inside the body.

Mr. Perkins was the patient lying on the x-ray couch. He was fully conscious, listening carefully to a nurse, who was holding his tightly clenched hand, while she explained everything that would happen. He was to have an examination called an Angiogram or Cardiac Catheterisation, one neither of us had ever seen so we too listened carefully to her explanation.

"Are you comfortable?" she asked her patient.

"Bit hard on me bum ain't it, but not to worry….. I've had worse beds than this," he managed between laboured breaths.

"OK! Well the doctor is going to make a small cut in your groin and push a long narrow tube up inside you, all along a blood vessel. We can watch it on the TV screen as it makes its way, right up to your heart. Then he will squirt some dye up it, which will look black on the screen to show us the inside of your heart and how well it is working. There will be lots of pictures taken and you will have to hold you breath and keep very still when they call to you. Is there anything you want to ask me?" she added.

"No 'ducks'…. just get on with it. I don't want to…. miss me lunch, almost worth all this…. just to get a change from the missus' bangers and mash…. after forty three years!"

Mr. Perkins laid his head back on the pillow, in spite of these severe heart problems exhausting him he still tried to face his fear with humour. One of the radiographers came over to instruct Joanna and me to stand behind the Consultant Radiologist, Dr. Wells, who was performing the procedure, so that we had a good view both of his actions and the television screen.

With deftly gloved fingers, he inserted the long flexible tube, stiffened with a guide wire, through the incision into Mr. Perkin's femoral artery and coaxed it carefully along its route to the main artery, the aorta, then through that blood vessel's arch, finally into the chambers of the heart. We watched spellbound as the catheter reached its destination. The guide wire was then removed, to allow the attachment of a pressurised syringe, prepared full of iodine, based 'dye,' to the exposed end of the catheter at Mr. Perkin's groin, ready to push the fluid into the tube.

Mr. Perkin's experienced nurse was caring for her patient with skill. He began to relax, beginning to release his knuckle-grinding grip on her hand, while he listened intently to her commentary. When the team acknowledged they were ready, the radiologist pumped hard his iodine filled syringe, causing a thin black streak to flow across the screen. Suddenly, whoosh the beating chambers of the heart were outlined for us all to see, as blood and 'dye' mingled into black-ribboned shadows, then streaking at speed quickly exited this vital organ to flow around the body.

It seemed instantaneous, almost too quick to follow, but with the next dose, a voice called out sharply, "Mr. Perkins, hold your breath!" while familiar exposure noises echoed in the room as frames of pictures were taken at a great rate recording the images on cine film.

Mr. Perkins suddenly exclaimed, "I can feel it, I can! Just like the missus says, a bloomin' hot flush all over. Oh my gawd!"

His nurse had for-warned him of the surge in body temperature when his circulatory system reacted to the presence of the 'dye' cascading through the blood vessels, on their journey to the various organs. Then the on-screen black shadow reached his kidneys, profiling his renal system actually doing its clearing out work, the black shadow flowed on, through the ureters, finally to his bladder, ready for excretion. What a wonderfully dramatic, cinematic performance!

Joanna and I were invited into the comparative calmness of Dr. Wells' office, as the Consultant Radiologist, examined his patient's developed series of films.

"Right girls, come closer. Here you can see Mr. Perkin's coronary arteries, the ones that give the heart its own blood supply. If they get completely blocked his heart will die, and so of course will **he**. What can you both see?"

Joanna, always the boldest, ventured, "I can see those two arteries outlined, but not too sure about any others."

"Well done, you are quite right," he praised her cheerfully. Then modifying his tone to a more serious timber he pointed to the images. "Unfortunately for Mr. Perkin's it looks as if two of his four coronary arteries are blocked, causing his heart to struggle and putting a great strain on it. In fact he is currently in heart failure, I'm sure you noticed his shortness of breath. He will need urgent surgery, which in itself is extremely risky. We are still in the early days of managing these conditions, but highly experienced surgeons are having to learn very quickly new techniques, which could give people a renewed chance of active life and, what's more, should give them a better quality life. However Mr Perkins has to help himself too, by giving up his forty a day smoking habit and finding a better diet than fried sausages and mash! Right you two, off you go and grab a cuppa, no doubt I will see quite a bit of you girls in the next two weeks."

"Thank you so much, it was amazing!" I gushed finding my voice at last, as we hurried out of the great man's office.

The senior radiographer we had seen briefly that morning was in the staff rest room.

"Oh, hello," she greeted us looking up with a smile, "I'm glad to see both of you have been watching the "angio". I hear it was a great success. Sorry I pushed you off so quickly this morning but I didn't want you to miss any of it. By the way I'm Doris, based in the general department but if you have any worries come and search me out."

Well I'd certainly got her wrong, thinking she had no time for novices like us.

"I don't know if you're interested," she continued, "but I have free tickets for the theatre tonight. Monday nights it's often difficult to fill all the seats, so many theatre companies hand out complimentary tickets for staff, at hospitals and police stations to use. These are to see Spike Milligan in "Son of Oblamov?"

"Wow!" exclaimed Joanna, " Great …but I don't suppose you have four, I don't mean to be greedy only the other two of our group are at Maida Vale and we wouldn't want to go without them?" she asked cautiously.

"I'll go and check with Susie our receptionist," Doris replied jumping up and hurrying out of the staff room.

"I do hope she doesn't think me rude, after such a friendly offer," worried Joanna.

"No, I'm sure not, you made it clear it was to be fair to the others," I reassured her, "anyway here she is coming back with an envelope in her hand."

"Well you're in luck there were five left, so you can take four and have a fun evening, it's supposed to be very funny and never the same two nights running."

We thanked her gratefully, looking forward to seeing Curtis' and Linda's faces when we revealed our good luck; Spike was one of the hugely successful, radio comedy group, along with Peter Sellars, Michael Bentine and Harry Secombe who formed "The Goons", a wonderful innovative show that our generation had all followed and he, particularly, had a reputation for creating its wacky humour.

We found Curtis and Linda already there.

"Our planned afternoon procedure was cancelled as the patient died a few hours earlier and there was no time to prepare anyone else," Linda told us. We explained about the show waving the tickets about to their delight, then hurriedly headed for our rooms to change.

Our seats were in the front row of the "Gods," as the highest seats above the stalls and the stage are nick-named. I felt sure I could touch the ceiling lights and looking down over the rail made me so dizzy I hung on to the back of my seat until the safety curtain was raised. When that curtain was lifted revealing the depth of the stage it seemed a less perilous height and as soon as Spike came on stage, all that was forgotten.

He was the master of ad-libbing, which meant none of his fellow actors had a clue what would happen next so the evening sped by with hilarious momentum. It was such a thrill to watch this great comic genius weave unrehearsed plot lines around his fellow actors, who amazingly adapted their performances to match Spike's inventiveness. I knew my brother James would be green with envy, as he and so many people never missed an edition of the "Goon Show", a masterpiece of radio entertainment. After the show I found I couldn't really explain what the play had been about but neither could the others, nevertheless we had laughed ourselves nearly sick and our ribs and stomach muscles ached for days. It was a brilliant antidote to some of the sad and serious cases we would be witnessing every day. No doubt that was why the staff of Hospitals and Police stations were given any spare tickets.

The Hammersmith Hospital's proximity to Wormwood Scrubs gave rise to some unbelievable radiographs.

"You must see these," said Amy, one of the junior staff, waving a couple of just developed films in our faces, in the wet viewing room the next morning. "This prisoner has been admitted with dreadful abdominal pain. Look here, no wonder he's doubled up and in agony, stupid man!" she declared. There, trapped in his abdomen, between his stomach and intestine were four teaspoons, which he had apparently, deliberately, swallowed at breakfast. By early afternoon he was being urgently prepared for major abdominal surgery having put himself into an emergency situation, for the longer these obstructions remained in his gut, the greater was the risk of a perforation in his small bowel and life threatening peritonitis.

"Sometimes they swallow pins when working in the mailbag room," Amy offered, "and even more bizarrely, we've had one daft enough to shove a carrot up his bum, which was not life threatening, but *he* certainly didn't enjoy having his bowel washed out with a hot soapy, pressurised enema, pretty uncomfortable!"

Apparently all sorts of ruses were concocted by prisoners desperate to be admitted for at least a week's respite from the harsh conditions of the "Scrubs". The promise of comfortable beds, pretty nurses and decent food, along with the chance to be treated as a patient not a prisoner was too tempting and it seemed many were prepared to take extraordinary risks with their health.

We were horrified; it had never occurred to either of us that prisoners would self-harm to that extent, even so a slightly wicked 'black humour' bubbled up seeing such unlikely ironmongery shining out from a black and grey abdominal x-ray. We realised that Curtis and Linda would also be regaled with these stories, and agreed to 'keep mum' so as not to spoil the radiographers' delight in shocking them, then enjoying their astonished reactions.

Our two weeks in the cardiology department sped by with new experiences everyday. It had felt so exciting to be at the sharp edge, witnessing many of these new techniques and procedures. Sadly it was over all too quickly, but fortunately we had managed to fill the requisite number of procedures in our log-books and many had been counter signed by the great man himself, Dr. Wells. Next stop Maida Vale.

Chapter 18

Dr. Wetherby sat at his desk in his small general practice surgery, studying the case notes of Colin Wilson. A knock rapped on the door and this same young man walked through into the consulting room.

"Hello Colin," greeted Dr. Wetherby with the familiarity of a family friend. He had known his patient since early childhood, which allowed an easy rapport between them, but even so, today there was a palpable tension about Colin's demeanour as he took the proffered seat.

"How are things?" the doctor continued.

"Not too good," was the reply. "The sight in my right eye seems worse than last week and I've been dizzy and sick with this wretched headache."

He had certainly lost more weight, thought Dr. Wetherby and his pallor accentuated the raw, redness of his right eye. All these factors were pointing towards a serious situation, which needed investigating further.

"I have a report here from the ophthalmologist you saw last Tuesday; he can find no problems actually within your eye, so we must look deeper than that. We have to find out if something is happening to your optic nerve or the eye's blood supply and for that I am referring you to Maida Vale Hospital, which specialises in the brain and nervous system, just in case there is a blockage somewhere in that area. I have an old friend and colleague, who is an expert in that field. His name is Mr. Shelby; we were at medical school together, where the other students called us the 'Two B's,' 'to be or not to be,'" he added with a wry smile trying to lighten this difficult consultation. "Colin, go back to the waiting room while I telephone old Shelby's secretary and fix up an appointment with him."

He ushered the anxious young man from the room and then picked up the shiny, black, telephone receiver from its cradle and dialled O. "Mavis put me through to Maida Vale please."

It was Joanna and my second day in the neurological x-ray department at this small highly specialised hospital, which attracted the expertise of surgeons and physicians from all over the world. We had spent the previous day studying endless x-rays of skulls, brains and spinal cords surrounded by text books, in the hope that we should at least have some understanding of what the forthcoming procedures were trying to achieve, which areas were being highlighted and what constituted beyond the range of normality. It was way outside anything we had studied so far, making us both anxious that if we should not succeed to grasp this work our ignorance may fail us when we reached examination level.

On Tuesday morning the 'specials room' was very busy as radiographers and nurses prepared for an imminent air encephalogram procedure. This complicated investigation was designed to examine the inside of the brain, trying to locate any tumours that might be present.

We crept in hoping to fade into the background but at once a doctor approached us.

"Good morning, I am Dr. Wetherby a local G.P., it is my patient who is having this x-ray today so I've been allowed in to watch the procedure as I've never seen one before. Are you two students?"

"Yes," replied Joanna, "and it's all new to us too."

"Shall we stand together?" asked Dr. Wetherby, "then explanations need only be aimed in one direction. I have to admit to being rather nervous, for my patient and for me," he added with a worried frown.

"Can you tell us a little about him?" asked Joanna, never one to hold back.

"I don't see why not, after all you have access to his case notes and you're here to learn. Colin Wilson is a thirty-year-old, policemen, who came to see me about a month ago with visual problems in his right eye and severe headaches with accompanying nausea. He was actually sick on duty one day and sent to the police doctor, who subsequently referred him back to me. Colin hasn't been on duty since."

"What do you think is wrong?" I asked, at last feeling comfortable with this pleasant G.P.

"I'm hoping that I'm wrong but I suspect a tumour, possibly pressing on his optic nerve, but we shall have to wait and see. Mr. Shelby the neurosurgeon caring for Colin was at medical school with me and agreed to let me stand in today."

At that point Colin was wheeled into the x-ray room looking shaky and apprehensive. Dr. Wetherby went straight over to help him out of the chair asking, "Colin, how are you?"

"Terrified!" the young man exclaimed.

"My dear boy, everyone here is on your side, wanting to get to the bottom of this problem. When I think what you face in the line of duty each day I know you will manage this ordeal." He patted Colin's shoulder, trying to reassure him as nurses helped him onto a special seat that was incorporated in the fancy x-ray equipment. They faced him away from us, exposing his thin frame with its knobbly spine, in readiness for a lumbar puncture.

Mr. Shelby and Dr. Haupsberg, the Consultant Radiologist, walked in, chatting together. They were both gloved and gowned as this was to be a sterile field, with sterile green towels draped around the working area that would encompass Colin's lower back and Dr. Haupsberg's lap.

"Mr. Wilson, Good Morning, I am going to perform a lumbar puncture on you in just a few moments," the radiologist began his lengthy explanation. "First of all I shall numb the area with local anaesthetic so you should not experience any discomfort after those initial scratches. I then have to push a special needle into your back. Once this hollow needle is in place some of your cerebral spinal fluid will drain out from your spinal sheath, allowing me to push a quantity of air through a syringe attached to the needle, to fill up its place. You are seated upright so that this air will then travel all the way up inside your brain. At that point we shall take some x-ray pictures. We need you to keep as still as possible throughout. Have you any questions?"

"No," was the single-worded reply.

Joanne and I had plenty, but knew that this was not the moment to seek answers.

We three spectators gathered behind Dr. Haupsberg's back as the now seated radiologist numbed Colin's lower back. Carefully he picked up the long, stainless steel, hollow lumbar puncture needle and pushed it hard into a gap between two bones low down in Colin's spine. Gently and very slowly he rotated the needle's stem until several large drops of clear cerebral spinal fluid plopped out. This was always a tricky procedure and as the doctor muttered, "I'm in," a collective sigh of relief murmured around the room. "Right we're on our way Mr. Wilson, soon be taking those vital pictures, just keep holding still you are doing very well."

An hour later we sat with Dr. Wetherby, each relishing a welcome cup of coffee.

"I feel very sad," he said quietly, almost to himself, "I've known Colin most of his life, watched him grow up a fine young man and become an excellent police officer." He paused for a moment sipping his hot drink, "Now he has to face the very real battle of surgery, then radiotherapy followed by rehabilitation, and that's if all goes well. The police career he longed for and enjoyed is now over for good. Survival and a quality of life will be all that matters. Mr. Shelby explained to me that the position of the confirmed tumour will make it difficult for its total removal and that anything left behind will probably grow again. But I'm afraid surgery is Colin's only option, he has no choice!" He looked at us sadly, conscious that we too had been badly affected by the result of the examination. "Girls that is what your future medical positions hold for you, some really good days and some as despondent as this. I wish you all the best with your studies and thank you for your support today."

He shook our hands and we watched this caring G.P. walk away, his shoulders slumped and his head down trying to grapple with

Mr. Shelby's bleak prognosis for Colin's future. These specialised hospitals dealt with the very serious cases that had been beyond other medical establishments; in the next two weeks we were going to witness devastating diagnoses and heartbreaking decisions.

Joanna and I returned to the B&B in subdued mood. We now understood why Linda and Curtis hadn't gone into much detail about the work at Maida Vale. Instead they had expounded on the lovely staff and great food, happy to let us chatter on about exciting heart cases at the Hammersmith x-ray department; for experiencing the neurological aspects of radiography work seemed completely different.

If the following days were going to be heavy, Joanna and I decided, then the evenings would need to lighten our load. We were young, free, let loose from parental suspicions and prying eyes, but although pretty poor, we could still stretch our finances as far as possible and "go out on the town". Obviously Linda and Curtis had come to the same conclusion as they stood in the hallway waiting for us to come in.

"Hi you two," greeted Linda, "We both fancy going dancing tonight, is there anywhere not too far and pretty cheap?" she clamoured.

"Well the Lyceum at Leicester Square has dancing to the latest juke box hits on a Monday and Tuesday so doesn't cost much, will that do?" Joanna answered, with a knowing grin at me, deciding this was exactly the right way to spend our evening.

"Great come on Curtis, back to the room and put your dancing shoes on while we girls get 'glammed' up," beamed Linda striding upstairs to our rooms.

We slipped into colourful mini-skirts and frilly tops, carefully pulled up the newly fashioned nylon tights, which meant stockings and suspenders could be suspended! No more fleshy thigh gaps exposed over the tops of poorly fitting stockings, now long smooth legs were covered high enough up to shock anyone over twenty, then placed on our feet spindly stiletto heeled shoes.

"Tonight is the night for a trial run," Joanna announced mysteriously as she huddled in front of the only mirror with two small hairy items resting in the palm of her hand.

"Can you two get out of the light I'm trying to put my false eyelashes on, I need to see where to put the glue."

"Come here," I said, "I'll do that and hand them to you, then you will have two hands free, one to keep your eye open and one to put the lash in the right place."

Together we managed to get them stuck in position. Next, her glasses were carefully rested in place. "Look," Joanna giggled, "They're sweeping the dust off the inside of my lenses."

"Hurry up you lot, I'm all done," Curtis shouted through the door. Linda opened it, "Wow look at you I didn't know you were a closet mod," she teased. He stood resplendent in a black polo neck shirt, dark single-breasted jacket with its 'mod-style' round collar, light tapered trousers and shiny pointed toe shoes. He inspected us all approvingly, delighted to have three, giggly girls hanging on his arms.

We joined the long, noisy queue of young people at the Lyceum, eagerly waiting to dance all evening to the hugely popular 'Liverpool Sound' that was sweeping the country. The ballroom was enormous, decked with red velvet drapes, while a gigantic, glass mosaic ball was spinning, suspended from the ceiling, scattering its rotating coloured rays of lights in sparkling beams across the gyrating heads of several hundred young men and women.

One hit Beatle tune followed another.

"Please, please, please me….." "Can't buy me love…" "She loves you yeah, yeah ,yeah…," echoed hundreds of voices in unison, arms waving in the air, bodies captured by the enveloping music as we bopped and twisted.

"Mary, quick," Joanna grabbed my arm, "urgent loo call!"

"What's up?"

"I've lost my left false eyelash, it crept down my cheek like a hairy centipede. I think it's in my top or bra," she gabbled urgently.

We dashed off the dance floor and to the amazement of the other occupants of the ladies, Joanna pulled off her top and thrust it in my hand while she scrabbled in her bra' and I examined her top.

"Here it is!" I cried, "Caught in the seam!"

We looked around at the astonished faces as I waved the 'little tufted beast' in Joanna's face, and collapsed with laughter. The perils of false anything, you never knew when you might be let down. Joanna pulled off the right set of lashes and stuffed them in her bag as we made our way back through the throng, still giggling.

It was a great evening, helping to push our patient Colin's sad situation from the forefront of our minds. Linda suggested that perhaps "hitting the town' was the only way Joanna and I would cope with any difficult cases that emerged during the next two weeks so we all resolved to seek out more enthralling evening entertainment.

Keeping to our new plan, the next night we found a coffee bar a few streets off from Leicester Square, which held live performance, music nights; no extra charge just the cost of our drinks.

Folk and Country & Western Music was becoming very popular here, wit American artists such as Johnny Cash and Julie Felix and the Irish group the Dubliners, Davy Graham, Ewan McColl, and many more emerging performers, competing with the flourishing pop-music world, so we were delighted to see posted on the door of this club:

"Visiting Troubadours, Buffy Sainte-Marie and Paul Simon,

Singing for your delight this evening."

We climbed down stone steps following a column of eager music fans into this dimly lit, smoky cellar. We girls just managed to grab a table with four small stools, while Curtis went off to get the coffees, which we hoped due to our financial state, would last all evening.

It took him some while, for by now the cellar was packed and the air heavy with smoke and sweat, as bodies became squashed against the walls with most young people standing, laughing and chatting all around the slightly claustrophobic room. It was pretty hot and noisy down there, but with the happy atmosphere of anticipation any uncomfortable feelings were quickly dispelled. Luckily our table was near the small performers' platform so no one crowded our small area of space and our view would not be impeded.

Suddenly an exotically dressed, American Indian lady bounded up to the platform and took the microphone between her heavily bangled hands, bouncing these colourful, enormous hoops around her wrists as she moved.

Buffy Sainte-Marie was of Native American Indian genealogy and as she began to sing her own haunting melody, "Universal Soldier", the whole cellar fell into total silence, which apart from applause wasn't breached for the next half hour, while we delighted in her absorbing music. Then she changed, upping the tempo so that her last few numbers beat out rhythmic pulses from her guitar, reverberating around the coffee bar. Tables were thumped in unison, spoons bashed together as everyone became engrossed in making their own contribution to the vibrant beat. She left the stage to shouts and cheers for more, but instead went to fetch her fellow musician, Paul Simon.

We had no prior knowledge of this young American singer, so we had no great expectations when this small, dark haired, rather ineffectual looking young man stood up to the microphone. Suddenly his voice took off and bound his audience together, everyone swaying as if under his control.

Most of these songs were his own composition. He had perhaps not yet developed to the stage of the most beautiful piece, 'Bridge over troubled water,' that he recorded in 1970, with his collaborator Art Garfunkel, which was to be such an enormous success placing them amongst the most famous international folk/pop artists of their time. However on this particular evening listening to him sing "The sound of silence," we knew that he would become something special. It felt so exciting to be sitting there in a small back street coffee bar, enveloped by rapturous audience applause, confident that this was the beginning of a momentous career.

The next two weeks marched on, proving to us the necessary work of radiographers at Maida Vale Hospital. They taught us the latest radiography techniques that were helping in the pioneering efforts to try and resolve brain and spinal conditions.

We watched in amazement as shunts were inserted into the brains of hydrocephalic children to drain off fluid and relieve the huge pressures and swellings in their brains. This new process had recently been invented by the engineering father of one of these affected children and was already proving successful. We witnessed trials to try and control the appalling tremors of Parkinson's disease: advances in surgical methods to remove tumours from the intricately positioned pituitary gland and other groundbreaking techniques. Some would develop further but some would be abandoned, the benefits too small and the risks too great. As this knowledge of neurological conditions and their treatments expanded around us it made headline news on the radio and in the press. Television brought these realities into our sitting rooms and doctors became celebrities, while we four students became carried along on the waves of excitement as these discoveries were being played out before us.

Chapter 19

Our four weeks brought us closer together and more confident with each other. We explored other musical places, confidently strolling our way about the back streets with their small coffee bars and intimate pubs.

One rainy evening we spent in a small, smoky club being entertained by a modern, Dave Brubeck style jazz group, the bass player thumping elusive rhythms which melted into the meandering of the pianist; new experiences for us all. Another found us squashed in a lively pub, packed with modern jazz fans collected together by the more traditional, Chris Barber, type jazz, for discovering this less well known London lifestyle was much more in line with our student pockets.

But many evenings we just sauntered round to our local, the 'Cat and Fiddle,' and it was there, in those familiar surroundings that we discovered much about each other.

On one occasion Joanna had arrived a little late, delayed by trying to find a telephone kiosk without a queue, to make a call home. She sat down with a heavy sigh and suddenly stated, "I needed to find out how my younger brother, Jamie has been coping. He is severely brain-damaged from birth. I don't know why I've never said anything before, suppose just wanting to hide that part of my life, but now I know you all really well it seems daft not to talk about him."

"How old is he?" asked the ever practical Linda.

"Fifteen now but he has a mental age of about four. Trouble is he is big for his age and strong, so when he has a four-year-old tantrum Mum and Dad can't cope. About six months ago they realised that they couldn't manage him any more and made the heartbreaking decision to place in him in residential care. The strain and tension between them had been awful, but since he's gone they are getting their lives back and each other. Jamie is now living on the other side of London. I try to get over to see him at weekends but if I can't I feel so guilty. I've stood up for him for so long, 'fighting his corner,' that's why I'm never frightened to speak out or ask questions and, as you've no doubt gathered, generally be rather vocal. However big he grows, I still feel responsible for him; he will always be my little brother. This time at Maida Vale has shown me how fragile the brain is, how easy it is for it to go wrong and I think it is helping me at last begin to accept Jamie for how he is; I know now I must face up to his permanent disability. He really isn't going to get any better; perhaps that's what I've finally accepted." She looked around at us and gave a weak grin. "You're a great sister," Curtis told her, "doing the best you can, so no more guilt trips eh!" "Curtis is always right," I added.

"Aren't I always!" he chipped in and the mood suddenly lightened. "I think we can stretch our finances to one more round of drinks tonight," he declared getting up to fetch another four glasses of lager and lime.

Linda was exactly as she was, a pretty but resolute young woman, determined to do well in everything she tackled. She was quiet but not the least bit shy, just didn't participate in "small-talk" preferring to sit back and listen.

Linda was an only child from a family that had lived for generations in a small village, where she had attended the same primary school as her parents and grandparents, moving on at eleven to the nearest town's Grammar school. She had a very steady boyfriend, Graham.

"How long have you and Graham been going out?" asked Curtis always interested in other peoples' 'love-lives'."

"Since school really, we just fit," she replied, then seeing the expression on his face, she continued, laughing. "Not in the way you are imaging by the look on your face. I'm still a virgin! Can you imagine our village, where everyone knows when you sneeze, what it would be like for my Mum and Dad if I got pregnant! I couldn't do it to them so best not to start what we couldn't stop."

"I admire your restraint and Graham's frustration!" teased Curtis.

"And so you should!" she retorted.

Curtis was as complicated as Linda was straightforward and very wary of letting any of us get too close, however the cosiness and intimacy of the 'Cat and Fiddle' somehow prompted me to try and find out more about him.

"You sometimes mention your Mum and sister but never your Dad, why?" I asked him that evening.

"Because I haven't got one, not alive anyway," he uttered quietly. I blushed, furious with myself for asking such a stupid and intrusive question. But it was said and I couldn't take it back.

Curtis saw my embarrassment and smiled a little. "He was killed when I was a child," he replied, "Dad was a government official in Kenya, where he, Mum and my little sister lived in an official residence with a chauffeur, nanny and a household staff. I was at boarding school here in England. Then one morning during the Guerrilla War, Dad was ushered into his car by the chauffeur to attend some very important meeting, but as the engine was started a bomb exploded under the vehicle. Devastation! Dad and his man were killed instantly! Mum and my sister had to pack up and come home, leaving his remains behind, buried there. So you see we don't even have a grave for him, it's as if he never existed. Not exactly a cheerful topic for evening chit-chat, eh Mary?"

I looked at him directly, holding his gaze, "I'm so sorry. It was a dumb thing to ask, but even so I'm glad you've told us," At last we girls now had an explanation for some of Curtis' dark moods that could sweep over him in an instance, when he distanced himself, withdrawing from everyone around.

"Right then Mary, now it is your turn to reveal all," ordered Curtis as he arrived back at the table with more drinks.

"Yes, I suppose so, but there's nothing really to tell, dull ordinary that's me," I grinned back at him.

"Come on, your Dad was in the London Police force and you lived over the Police Station, that's hardly ordinary," he persisted.

"Mum and Dad were very good and allowed me out to the nearest dance halls with my friend and we were always at the pictures, but I was nearly sixteen and in spite of that freedom still awkward and shy. Unlike most of my classmates I had never had a boyfriend, which set me up for constant teasing and I was finding that hard to ignore. Anyway there's my excuse for doing the stupidest thing ever!"

"Well you've got us hooked now,' said Linda, "out with it, whatever did you do?"

"My aunt (the one I lived with when I first came to Elmbridge) Mum's eldest sister was staying with us at the time, a factor in this pathetic saga." I explained, "Anyway one evening, just as I had got off the bus from the local dance hall, some lads in a car pulled up beside me, right outside the entrance gates to the police station. One of them leant out of the window and called me over, "Hey, do you want to go to the pictures tomorrow? Do you live here?" he asked.

I said I did, then the thought struck me, yes a date, I can say I've got a date; that'll stop them all getting at me all the time. "OK," I said impetuously.

"Right then I'll meet you over the road at the bus stop, 7.00 pm. I'm Barry, what's your name?"

"Mary," I answered, then quickly turned away and ran up all the flights of stairs to our flat feeling both excited and scared.

"What did you tell you Mum, did you say you got 'picked-up'?" asked Linda.

"Mum called out to ask me how the dance had gone as soon as I got in, so I knew I had to tell her. "Oh, by the way I met this nice lad Barry there, he's taking me to the pictures tomorrow at seven." I tried to say casually, but I was hopeless at lying and I knew she didn't quite believe me; anyhow she just smiled and said that sounded nice. I went straight to bed to avoid any more questions not knowing she and my aunt would sit up for hours worrying and trying to work out what to do. Mum had a good idea what was I was suffering at school and realised that an actual date was very important to me.

Next day at school, I announced I had met a lovely bloke Barry and we were off to the pictures that evening. It certainly caused a stir and I began to wonder what I had done accepting an almost "blind date" but it seemed already to be doing the trick, I was "joining that elusive club."

That evening, I dressed carefully, not my shortest skirt, not my tightest jumper and not too much eyeliner. Mum and aunty looked me over. Satisfied I didn't look 'tarty' they let me go. What I didn't know until later was that they were right behind me!

I ran down the stairs half hoping he wouldn't be there, but sure enough standing by the bus stop stood a shortish, spotty youth with quiffed greased hair, wearing "winkle-picker' shoes.

He said "Hello," and handed me a small box of Dairy Box Chocolates with a broad smile.

I thanked him, nicely, but oh my God, "He's got bad teeth and bad breath," was all that sped through my brain. Apparently Mum and Aunty had crept across the road, between the traffic and hidden behind the nearby telephone kiosk. They must have looked ridiculous, bent double, spying at Barry and me through the glass windows."

"How on earth didn't you see them?" laughed Joanna.

"I reckon I was too busy trying to work out how not to kiss someone with bad teeth!" I giggled back. "It appeared Mum wanted to intervene but aunty convinced her he looked pretty harmless and that their parents had had no idea what Mum had got up to at nearly sixteen, when she had been in service hundreds of miles from home. So after watching us get on the bus, Mum returned reluctantly to the flat to wait several anxious hours until I came home."

I looked questioningly at the other three but they urged my saga on.

"It was an unremarkable Doris Day film and I held his hand, just for show, but really it was a pretty disastrous date.

We got back to the station gates and he asked, "Are you a policewoman?"

So then I realised he must have been on a dare, that's what this was all about. I told him no, I was still at school thinking great, that what will kill off any of his interest. Instead, to my horror he decided that he would meet me the next morning, in my school uniform, at

8.00 a.m. and walk me to the bus stop. He gave me a peck on the cheek and strolled off. I ran up the stairs in a total panic. I called out, it had been a nice evening and goodnight to Mum, as I couldn't face her and flung myself angrily on my bed.

No, no, no I did not want to go out with him again. What a fool I'd been just trying to stop the other girls baiting me. I couldn't sleep so I planned my escape. To Mum's surprise I was up early the next morning, I told her and aunty the truth about how we had met and how I couldn't possibly meet up with Barry and what I had decide to do. I was going to creep through the station garage, situated right under the building out of sight, which housed all the police cars and run up its slope the other side to catch a really early bus to school. They both agreed and hurried off to watch out from the dining room window to see if he turned up. He certainly wouldn't want to hang around for long, Mum decreed, once a few burly policemen showed an interest in him."

"Did he turn up?" asked Curtis,

"Yes Mum said he only stayed five minutes, thank goodness before heading off and I never saw him again."

"I didn't know you had such a mean streak, Mary," teased Curtis, "What a waste of a box of chocolates and a cinema ticket, all for a peck on the cheek. You were such a rotter Mary, what a real hussey!" laughed Curtis as Linda and Joanna both joined in, picturing me slinking off to school to get away from a spotty youth with bad breath; hardly the date I had dreamed of.

"Come on girls all this confessing is thirsty work. Lets go mad and have another round of drinks," grinned Curtis, much happier at the jollity and altogether lighter mood we had at last created. In fact so merry had we become, that he eventually escorted three very tiddly giggly, girls back to our B & B, for it took a lot more than four lager and limes to get an ex naval cadet blotto.

I like to think these confidences were shared because of the growing affection and respect we were developing between us, but the closeness of the past four weeks was almost at an end, for in a couple of days we would be returning to Elmbridge.

Our last Friday of freedom arrived but instead of dashing home we decided to splash out our remaining money on a celebratory meal at Lyons Corner House, in the Strand. We collected our baggage from No. 33and said goodbye to Mrs. Eames then made our way to the station to dump our stuff at the left luggage office before heading off to the restaurant.

Dressed in our best we were ushered to a white linen clothed table, with a single red rose adorning the centre, by a trim, pretty waitress. She wore a black uniform dress, topped by a white, starched lace-edged apron and a frilly cap perched precariously on her mop of dark hair, cut in the high fashion, 'bob' style of Mary Quant. Once seated we studied the menu together, but although we tried to assume airs of sophistication most of the dishes were beyond our experience, so when our waitress returned we all decided to order "Scampi and Chips in a Basket," a gimmicky new way of presenting this popular dish.

A pianist played his grand piano in the corner surrounded by artificial palm trees, capturing the phrase, "Palm Court Music." There was a sprung dance floor in the centre of the room where couples showed off their elegant skills at the Quickstep or the Foxtrot between courses, all very gentile.

Our meal arrived. The Scampi and Chips nestled in a doyley-lined wicker basket with a slice of lemon to garnish and a small pot of tartar sauce in the corner. As this was to be "finger food" our waitress produced four pairs of plastic disposable gloves, which to her astonishment caused us all to burst out in loud laughter, causing curious looks from the occupants of neighbouring tables. These were exactly the same gloves that we had to wear when pushing an enema catheter up a patient's rectum, hardly the expected accessories for a luxury meal in such tasteful surroundings. No doubt the accrued tension from the difficult and sometimes traumatic cases we had recently witnessed needed to escape and spilled over in all this hysterical hilarity at Lyons Corner House, eating Scampi and Chips with plastic enema gloves.

"It's been a great four weeks," said Joanna as we collected our left luggage. "I can't imagine how dull Miss South's Youth Hostel would have been. We've been so lucky just the four of us, sharing luxuriously served breakfasts, washed down with watered down fruit juice, dining on ten baked beans every morning. I've been kicked black and blue by Mary; made tiddly by Curtis and kept sane by Linda. I think we've learned an enormous lot but even better, lived a lot too. Oh! My train leaves in five minutes, see you Monday. Thanks for a fantastic time." She hugged us all and grabbed her suitcase, dashing off, while we turned to scan the timetable for the next train back to Elmbridge.

It was time to go home.

Chapter 20   April 1965

Ted poured the last drops of custard on to his treacle tart then looked across the table at his wife.

"Grace, I've decided, I've had enough!" he declared.

"What enough treacle tart? I should think so that's your second slice."

"No, no, I'm packing it in at the hospital!" he retorted.

"What on earth has brought that on?"

"Well me back's been playing merry hell since I pushed that ruddy portable machine up the corridor, when its motor packed up, and to tell the truth it's not been the same since old 'bumbly' Petrie's been in charge," he explained.

"You've missed the little Sister haven't you, always had a way with her, you did," his wife teased.

"Yeah, she was a little firecracker, but never with me; we rubbed along fine."

"Well if you've decided… I'm not sorry really, be nice to have the odd day out or walk in the park or just sit in the garden together. I'm ready for it, been waiting for you to be ready that's all. When will you leave?" she asked eagerly.

Ted got up from the table, "I'll give me notice in tomorrow, then leave about the end of the month, give them time to sort something out. I'll go and draft me resignation letter now," he added, moving across to the bureau and pulling out writing paper, pen and envelope. "Shan't need a stamp I'll put it on old 'bumbly's' desk, in the morning, before he gets in."

Leslie had just returned home from an important visit to her Doctor's evening surgery. Brian, her husband, had got back from his duties at the hospital and was already busy in the kitchen putting the kettle on for coffee, when he saw her walk through the door.

"Wow look at you!" he admired, "you look as beautiful as the day we met, your eyes are sparkling and there's even a glowing flush on your cheeks. Am I right, did it go well?"

She threw her arms around him and hugged him tightly. "Yes my darling, wonderful news, I'm about ten weeks gone, we're definitely having a baby!" A few happy tears dampened her cheeks and moistened his, while they clung happily to each other.

Brian stepped back, still holding her in his arms, but now with a serious face, which calmed their euphoria for a moment. "Leslie, ionising radiation is very dangerous to a tiny forming foetus, I mean *our* baby. You must stop work immediately!"

"I know, don't worry, I'm never going near another x-ray, now I'm pregnant. I will hand in my notice tomorrow; work the last month checking films at the sorting bench, we…." she patted her still flat tummy, "will be perfectly safe there. I can even sit down all day if I want to. I will write my letter of resignation after we've eaten, then we can settle down and discuss what we need for this little person."

Letitia and Dr. John Meredith were deep in the discussion of their wedding plans. The church and reception venue had been chosen and booked, but the photographer and the bridal cars still had to be arranged.

"Oh! and another thing, I haven't ordered the flowers to decorate the inside of the church, my bouquet and the bridesmaids posies are already sorted, so please add the church's needs onto the list," Letitia asked her fiancé.

"Here," John replied, suddenly handing her a previously opened envelope, "you need to read my letter of confirmation for the Surgical Registrar's post at Winchester."

She took it eagerly and read it carefully through twice, then beaming at him Letitia said, "That's decided then! I'll give my notice in tomorrow so that I can devote my time to the details of the wedding and we can go down to Winchester, when you're off duty, to look for a house or flat to rent. I'm not needed at the moment anyway, while they install the new fangled, imaging equipment and T.V. monitor, into the screening room. There won't be any Barium work in the department for about three weeks and when there is, it will most likely become the work of only qualified radiographers', I'd rather leave before I'm pushed! Pass me a pen John, please, I'll draft out my letter of resignation and you can check it for me. Can't say I'll even miss it, old 'bumbly' Petrie's a real pain; it's never been the same since Sister Aster left," then taking the proffered pen, Letitia hurried off in search of some headed writing paper.

Martin was sitting by himself at the bar of 'Ward 9,' generally known as 'The Hospital Arms,' huddled over a pint mug of beer. Earlier that evening he and Sister Jane had at last decided to break off their long-standing relationship. It really wasn't going anywhere and lately he had suspected she was seeing someone else, so best to make it look like a mutual decision, that way no one lost face.

To be honest he was totally 'brassed-off,' for in addition, working under 'bumbly' Petrie was disastrous, this job was going nowhere; his delight at promotion to Deputy had become a total disappointment.

It seemed to Martin that he had less authority now, than before as a senior, working under Sister Aster; his every suggestion was thwarted by that little wimp of a man, who had turned out to be incredibly stubborn and incapable of delegation.

Martin leaned across the bar to Tom, who pulled another beer and handed the foaming pint to Martin, who announced, bitterly, " I've decided, I'm going to take that job at Stourwater Hospital, it's just what I need, get away, right away from him and from her!"

"Didn't know you had another job lined up," replied Tom, rather surprised.

"Yeah, applied last month, but I held on to see what Jane was up to. The interview went well, just got to let them know my decision by next week. Trouble is I love Elmbridge and all the other things I do here; hockey, charity group, tennis in the summer, so it's a wrench to leave, but somehow I think now is the right time to go. I'll trot off home and write my resignation letter and delight in putting it on old 'bumbly's' desk tomorrow!" He quickly downed his pint and with a determined stride set off home.

Mr. Petrie's day had begun badly. It had taken him ten minutes to locate his car keys hiding down the side of his battered old armchair. Next the dustcart sat blocking his driveway while the troublesome old lady from across the road, berated one of the dustmen.

"You missed me last week!" she expounded. "A fox tipped over the bin and I had rubbish everywhere!"

"You put it out too late," retorted the muscular crew leader, and so it went on until Mr. Petrie managed to attract their attention to his plight. Relieved at a diversion the harassed dustman instructed his driver to move the lorry and as it pulled away he leapt eagerly into the cab, squashing up with his three mates.

Free at last Mr. Petrie set off for the hospital only to join a queue of vehicles trying to negotiate a difficult crossroads where the traffic lights had seized up on red; just about the colour his state of mind had reached.

Fifteen minutes late he arrived hot and breathless at his office door. With a swift "Good morning" to Brenda at reception, he closed the door behind him and hung his coat firmly on its peg.

Then he saw them, four different sized, different coloured and very different handwritten envelopes, all stamp less, obviously hand delivered and all bearing his name and title.

Mr. Petrie, Superintendent Radiographer, X-ray Department, Elmbridge Hospital.

He fingered them carefully, placing them in a pile with a strange feeling of foreboding and picked up his telephone receiver.

"Brenda, no calls or disturbances for at least half an hour, unless really urgent!" Then slowly he picked up the top letter and slid a paperknife under the flap, reluctantly extracting a single sheet of paper. This was not going to be a good day!

Although we were all severely shocked by the planned mass exodus from the department, our student lives had reached a crucial stage, for we were all working at fever pitch towards the Part 1 Examinations, which started in two days time. Every hour was spent pouring over notes, text books, practising formulae and equations and trying to draw complex anatomical diagrams from memory. To achieve that necessary level of concentration, we were closeted away from the department upheaval and gossip, in the radiographers' sitting room.

"It's no good I will never remember the structure of the eye!" wailed Joanna, "it's OK for you and Linda, Mary, you're both good at drawing but my effort looks more like an emblem for nuclear disarmament."

"Yeah, but you're not so fazed by the Physics, my atoms, equations and formulae are so confused," I complained not to be out done.

"Oh! Stop it you two, let's have some hush," demanded Curtis as he handed out some supposedly calming cigarettes.

Linda kept her head down and sensibly ignored the panicky voices surrounding her as she continued scribbling page after page from memory.

Two days later, Linda, Curtis and I sat silent and tense on the early commuter train to London. Our destination was The Examination Halls, Russell Square WC1. Curtis had brought his large Grey's Anatomy in his brief case and retrieved it for study during the journey. To my surprise he had it opened at the detailed description and diagram of the tongue, an organ and area that we had never been taught.

"What ever do you want to know about that for?" I snapped derisorily.

"I know," he replied, his voice heavy with sarcasm, " it's an area for therapy radiography students, but don't forget we share the anatomy paper and I can chose from any of the six questions, so just shut up and leave me alone!"

We met Joanna outside the red-bricked, Georgian styled building, and then armed with our exam numbered entrance cards, we crossed the threshold to join a queue. Slowly, we filed silently into the huge hall to be greeted by the familiar examination layout of row upon row of desks, well spaced to prevent any chance of cribbing.

Once seated I looked at the large clock hanging on the end wall, it was 9.24 a.m. and there on the desk before me was a plain sheet of green paper, waiting to test my knowledge and recall capabilities. Suddenly a powerful voice interrupted my nervous conjectures.

"You have one and a half hours to complete this paper on Physics. Your five minutes reading time starts now."

The room stirred with multiple rustlings of paper as the green sheets were flipped over to reveal five closely typed questions, from which, three had to be answered.

"Oh! Thank goodness," I breathed to myself, for Question no. 2 asked that a 'fully labelled diagram of the structure of an x-ray tube' be drawn, along with a description of how x-rays were produced. At least there was one I could answer.

"You may commence writing. Time starts now!" resounded the command.

"Pens down now!" insisted that same voice exactly one and a half hours later. After a short break the whole process was repeated for the second of the three subjects, Hospital Practice. At last came the lunch break, when we were able to get together and compare our morning's hopes and despairs.

"I really can't eat anything, I feel so sick," I whinged.

"Come on Mary, of course you can, we can't have you embarrassing us by fainting during the Anatomy Paper," insisted the ever practical Linda.

"Here have one of my sandwiches," urged Joanna handing me one from her plate.

Curtis said nothing as he continued his study of the tongue.

Once more seated at our desks in the Hall, we turned over our Anatomy Paper on command. Six questions lay written before us, and yes, of course there it was, No 4. 'Describe the function of the tongue with an accompanying fully labelled diagram.' I glanced across at Curtis who returned my incredulous expression with a very smug smile.

Chapter 21

I was going to be late, having overslept once again, when I bumped into the postman on our doorstep. He handed me a long brown official looking envelope, which to my surprise was addressed to me. As I thanked him it suddenly registered that it was six weeks since the examinations in London; this must contain my results.

I let myself back in the house and sat weakly on the stairs, turning the envelope over and over in my hands.

"Mum my results have come," I shouted up to her.

"Oh! What does it say? Have you passed dear?" she asked eagerly.

"Don't know, haven't opened it yet."

"Well for goodness sake do so!" she chided running down the stairs to sit beside me.

I carefully lifted the flap and slid out a single sheet of white paper.

"Wonderful, darling," she read over my shoulder, "you've passed all three papers. We'll have a celebratory meal tonight, perhaps open a bottle of wine," and hugged me so tightly I could scarcely breathe.

"Yeah that would be great. Gosh, I've got to get off, see how the others have done. Bye." I grabbed my bicycle and pedalled furiously to the hospital.

Curtis, Linda and Joanna stood at the bottom of the corridor, waiting for me. Then we were hugging and dancing around with excitement; not one failure at Elmbridge, Mr. Petrie's face was a wonder to behold, no one had ever before seen such a huge smile of delight light up his impenetrable features. We were half way there.

The following Friday, Leslie, Martin, Ted and Letitia were given a joint send-off from the "Hospital Arms." Leslie was presented with a rattle and fluffy toy for her expected baby, Ted a rose bush for his collection, Martin had been very tricky so in the end he received a book token and Letitia was given a Wedding Photo Album, after generous donations from the three radiologists. Collecting the requisite money for four leavers had been a nightmare and everyone felt "given-out!"

With our collective set of exam results to celebrate, it was a both a happy and poignant evening; Martin especially faced leaving with mixed emotions. He knew that in his present circumstances moving on was inevitable but disappointing, for only a few months earlier his promotion had brought more money and he had visualised a possible future with Sister Jane.

Leslie and Letitia were both excited about their life changes and even Ted beamed with pleasure at the thought of tending his roses.

But one other member of staff was unaccounted for; the whereabouts of Marsa was causing concern. She had taken three weeks annual leave to visit her brother, who was working on the south coast somewhere, however she was due to be back on duty the Monday before Leslie and Martin left.

Marsa had never revealed any details about her life outside the department. She did her work efficiently and politely, then in the evenings, except taking a bed in the nurses' home when on-call, she returned to her rented flat. In the time I had known her, since cadetship, I had never seen anyone break down the shield she had built around herself, no one got near, no one got close because no one was allowed to become her confidant. However, now it was worrying, her return date had been passed with no contact from her at all.

Mr. Petrie consulted the Personnel Department, who had her brother's address, but as he was not connected to the telephone, they could only write to him and wait for his reply. During the second week of her unexplained absence, Mr. Petrie called as many of us as he could together in the staff rest room.

"It's about Marsa, um…..personnel have um… heard from her brother," he began. "He claims…..um.. Marsa was very unhappy here. I…I didn't know that. Did.. did any of you?" Everyone looked at each other and shook their heads, but she was inscrutable, we rarely saw her cheerful, if ever; it seemed impossible for anyone to gauge her recent emotional state for if she had been unhappy she certainly hadn't made any protest. He continued "Her brother says she has left the country…. gone home, Personnel don't know um…. which country home is," Mr. Petrie continued. "We've no way of tracing her…. um…. so we shall have to appoint…. um…. another radiographer," he concluded, sounding weary and worried.

This loss of staff was becoming a difficult issue especially for him and now the accusation of an unhappy radiographer, after several years of presumably content employment, reflected badly on his management skills. This role of Superintendent Radiographer was not working well for the little grey man. And what had really happened to Marsa, we never knew, it became a mystery that was never solved.

Mr. Petrie now had to his biggest challenge yet, to staff the multiple vacancies in the department. The Management Committee insisted they were only looking for young newly qualified staff to fill the two junior posts, those who would have been trained in the latest techniques. Many of the pioneering radiographers of the 1930's and 40's were retiring, their knowledge now outdated as more and more complex procedures were being developed. Jeanette was wisely promoted to Deputy Superintendent and Mr. Petrie at last delegated to her all the personnel management duties. Her calm, positive influence settled the anxious upheaval surrounding us all, while these new staff members were being recruited. Two senior positions were also advertised, again desiring radiographers with the minimum years of service.

One afternoon Jeanette came over to the sitting room, while we were at study.

"Now that you are on your way to taking part 2 in November, which is only a few months away. I need to ask you three about your aspirations. What ideas have you got for employment when you pass?" She addressed this request to Linda, Joanna and Curtis, as I would have to wait six more months until my twentieth birthday, in the following April, to take Part 2.

"I have asked around locally, and St. James' Hospital near me, want me to apply as soon as I qualify," Joanna replied looking anxiously at us for our reactions to this news.

"Good, that makes sense, well done for looking ahead. What about you two, Curtis and Linda, have you any thoughts?"

"You first," Curtis nodded to Linda.

"Thanks. Well I hoped if there was a position to stay on here and gain experience, especially in on-call duties. It would be good to feel confident in my surroundings and be familiar with the equipment until I have got more used to working those duties single-handed," explained the ever practical Linda.

"Yes that's probably a wise decision. And Curtis how do you feel?"

"Pretty much the same as Linda. This should be a life-time career for me if everything works out well so I need to be really confident before I move onwards, and hopefully upwards," he added grinning, knowing Jeanette would respect his ambitions.

"That is pretty much what I expected. Mr. Petrie is planning to increase the number of juniors about November time to meet with the new screening facilities, which are nearing completion. The Society has insisted that only qualified staff can be employed and with the larger number of patients planned to attend each session we will have to boost our radiographic entail," Jeanette concluded.

"I haven't forgotten you Mary, just not your time yet is it?" She said kindly as she walked out of the door. I gave her a weak smile feeling unreasonably jealous of my compatriots, it seemed a distance was already growing between us.

Preparatory lectures for Part Two examination resumed at Brunswick Hospital with three new subjects delivered by the amazing hotchpotch of tutors only Miss South could employ.

She taught the Radiographic Technique session with her usual efficiency, but had secured a chain-smoking, dishevelled and rather bitter Ilford Films sales representative to conduct out Photography tuition. He typically arrived late and was anxious to leave as soon as was permissible. We discovered he had been a radiographer but had never achieved promotion to senior level, so the paltry pay of a junior radiographer was never going to procure him a mortgage, hence his reluctant diversion into the commercial world of 'sales.'

He moaned constantly about his life "on the road" and appeared to view our prospective interesting and fulfilling careers with resentment; we still had the opportunity to achieve where he had failed. Consequently his lectures were terse, factual but uninspiring.

The second tutor Miss South introduced us to a Hospital Secretary from Brunswick's small, out of town, isolation hospital. He was an eccentric gentleman dressed totally in green, mixed tweed with heavy horn-rimmed spectacles perched vulnerably on his short stubby nose. His addition to instructing our education came from his hobby, dismantling old x-ray equipment. He lectured us in the third discipline for Part Two, Apparatus Construction. To his credit he was extremely enthusiastic about the subject, covering the blackboard with extensive diagrams and littering the tables with parts of x-ray tubes and high-tension cables but his knowledge of the new, innovative imagery equipment we had worked with in London was sparse. Our day release to Brunswick became more of a burden than benefit, so yes, it was back to textbooks, latest approved papers and Elizabeth's marvellous notes.

Since Martin's departure, and because he was now well into his second year of training, Curtis was allocated most of the x-ray examinations of the male nether regions, monitored of course by Mr. Petrie, but he liked to keep his distance as such examinations proved too intimate for this introverted gentleman's 'hands-on' involvement.

Curtis arrived one morning to be greeted by Mr. Petrie standing anxiously at the bottom of the corridor.

"Curtis hurry up, we have an urgent urethrogram to do as quickly as…. um…. possible. I have set the room up and the…. um…. gentleman is…. changing."

Curtis looked at us three girls, as we listened in to Mr. Petrie's orders, in surprise, it was most unusual to have such a request for a special procedure so early in the day.

"Right, OK I'll get him started. Do you have the request form?" he replied.

Mr. Petrie handed over the patient's information card for Curtis to peruse. "Oh my God! What an idiot!" Curtis breathed out. "I can't believe any one would be so desperate to do that!"

Filled with curiosity we crowded round to see what had caused this outburst.

Under reason for x-ray request the examining urologist had written:

Emergency Casualty Admission 6.30 a.m.

This patient suffered severe lower abdominal pain following complete urinary retention.

Unable to pass any urine for the last 12 hours.

To try to relieve his situation the patient has inserted a Biro refill into his urethra and pushed it up as high as possible, instead of widening the aperture and canal these are now completely blocked. The refill now lodges somewhere in his penis which has swollen around it. Please locate prior to surgery.

We looked at each other in astonishment, no wonder Mr. Petrie had passed this case to Curtis, as he probably couldn't even bring himself to discuss such action let alone perform the procedure.

Curtis grinned at us girls, "Well I never expected my naval experiences to come in so handy, nothing men do surprises me anymore. OK! Let me get the poor blighter in and get started, he must be in agony!" Later that morning a biro refill was retrieved, bagged and joined, 'Unusual artefacts discovered in surgery,' in the hospital medical library.

Within a few weeks three new staff members joined the department. The two juniors were newly qualified from Northern Ireland. Both had been trained at Newry General Hospital and had become great friends. They had particularly wanted positions in England but had resolved to stay together so to our good fortune we gained Colette and Anna, whose Irish charm beguiled us all from their first day. The senior staff replacement was Mavis, a single rather austere person with a conscious attitude of authority, which when both attributes were combined they produced a less than pleasing manner.

Curtis Linda and Joanna were in 'panic mode' as they had only four months left to not only absorb all the knowledge they could, but complete the requisite number of examinations for their log books. I felt left out of this frenzy and unreasonably cheated, although of course I had always known my six months lack of age would render it this way.

Naturally enough they grabbed all the more obscure cases for their records, "You've still got plenty of time Mary!" which again pushed me to one side.

They took extra study time, while I was seconded to the nearby Geriatric Hospital to become an expert in x-raying arthritic hips, 'bad back' and stiff necks, all very useful but not very exciting.

I am sad to say, but have to truthfully admit, I was extremely jealous.

Chapter 22

Laura stood quietly at the reception desk watching me as I studied my watch with a heavy sigh. It was 8.40 a.m. Curtis, Linda and Joanna would be nervously filing into the multi-desked, examination hall at Queen's Square, adrenaline flowing, eager to get on with the daunting day ahead.

Part Two examinations were awaiting their attention.

"Come on Mary," Laura urged, "only six months to wait and that will fly by, anyway we have a 'special' this morning, perfect for your log book, a Micturating Cystogram. Let's go and get set up for the patient, who must be feeling so anxious."

Laura had recently filled the remaining vacant senior position, her personality and attitude a refreshing contrast to Mavis. She was a lively, sophisticated young woman in her late twenties, middle-height with a fashionable chestnut bobbed style of hair, framing arched shaped eyebrows and bright hazel eyes that currently probed my dismal demeanour, forcing my mood to lighten and fire a spark of interest in the morning's planned proceedings.

Mrs. Davis waited nervously in the x-ray corridor, she knew this investigation would be awkward, difficult, even embarrassing, but there was nothing to be done she couldn't go on as she was. She was a dumpy lady in her late forties, who had been delivered of five full-term babies and two failed pregnancies, which had weakened her pelvic floor muscles so much, that with every sneeze, cough, sudden laugh she peed; not a lot but enough to wet her pants, it was humiliating!

Mrs. Davis had constantly practised the exercise regime taught to her by one of the physiotherapists but there had been little improvement so the urology consultant had referred her for a pre-operative x-ray procedure, the resulting surgery should help him make the necessary adjustments to her bladder and urethra, thereby hopefully restoring full urine control to his patient.

"Mary can you get our patient changed please?" requested Laura. I fetched a clean, starched, white gown from the linen cupboard and approached the solitary, plump lady sitting in a brown, gabardine raincoat, perched stiffly on the edge of her chair.

"Hello, Mrs. Davis, come with me and let's get you changed," and I handed her the white gown as I led her to the changing cubicles.

In the x-ray room Laura waited by a sterile trolley laid out with the necessary equipment.

'Mary you learnt how to catheterise a patient in your ward training didn't you?' she queried.

"Yes I've done it several times, shall I see to Mrs. Davis then?" I asked.

"Fine you scrub up while I explain to her what we are going to do," she replied. I headed off to the sink and the waiting nailbrush, to soap my hands with the foaming antiseptic hand wash, then powdered them before pulling on thin, sterile rubber gloves.

Laura approached our seated patient.

"Good morning Mrs. Davis, let me explain this procedure to you. Firstly there will be only Mary and myself involved all the way through, your privacy is assured; Mary will put a fine catheter into your bladder and we will fill it with a fluid that x-rays can't pass through, often called a 'dye,' but it is colourless and doesn't stain anything. When your bladder is completely full you will sit up on this raised bench, sideways to the x-ray plate and empty your bladder into the receptacle positioned below."

"Do you mean actually pee when I'm perched up there?" Mrs. Davis whispered horrified, looking up at the bench balanced on the table-top of our, securely braked, portable x-ray couch, the only way the x-ray plate could be lined up at the right level against her as she peed.

"Yes, I'm afraid so, but we need a picture of you actually passing urine to see why you leak it when you don't want to. I'm sorry, it's such a crude set up but so far no one's come up with a better way of getting the information your consultant needs before he can operate." Laura took her hand and squeezed it tightly as she smiled assuredly into Mrs. Davis face, "Believe me we are both on your side and will help you all the way, for neither Mary nor I would want to have to do your bit, but it will be worth it when you can go out and about confidently once more, trust us we will make it as bearable as possible."

The dear lady managed a weak smile and climbed up on the couch ready for me to pop the catheter in, which thankfully proved amazingly easy. Laura then filled her bladder until Mrs. Davis announced she was bursting and ready to climb once again, this time up to be seated on the bench beside the x-ray plate. She looked very vulnerable as she shuffled back as far as possible, so that her posterior overhung the waiting receptacle, but more importantly her bladder and urethra had to be away from the obscuring wood of the bench, as she hung on to the film carriage with the opposite hand, her arms across her chest to stop her toppling off (*Health and Safety officials would have nightmares today, no wonder this procedure soon became obsolete!*).

I positioned the x-ray camera at Mrs. Davis hip level, in line with the film on her other side so that we could capture both the internal bladder and the external flow of urine.

With our patient perched in such an inglorious fashion, Laura and I quickly retreated behind the protective screen to the control panel.

"Ok, Mrs. Davis, when you're ready, we're all set for action so pee away any time now," instructed Laura.

"I'm trying," came the response…….nothing happened!

"Give a cough!" instructed Laura.

Mrs. Davis gave a raspy smoker's cough…….nothing happened!

"See if you can sneeze!" implored Laura.

"Atishoo!"………nothing happened!

"Can you laugh dear?" tried Laura.

"Well I bet I look a sight stuck up here," she retorted with a false laugh but still the receptacle remained empty.

"Let's turn on the taps Mary," declared Laura, so I rushed to the sink and turned on the running, tinkling sound of water splashing into the basin.

After a few minutes Laura looked at me and we both burst out laughing, "Please Mrs. Davis, Mary and I are crossing our legs behind her, we could both do it for you!"

With that our precariously placed patient burst out laughing, calling out, "It's working, I'm peeing girls!"

"Hold your breath and keep still," called Laura as she made the exposure for our one shot chance at getting it right; it had to be good, for once the receptacle was full there was no going back.

As I ran the film round to the darkroom Laura helped our lovely patient down from her undignified perch and gave her a big hug. I returned with the film, which showed the white shadow of her filled bladder as it released its white, ribboned stream of fluid, forming an image that captured both the internal and external functions perfectly. Success!

Mrs. Davis returned to her cubicle to get dressed then thanked us both for our care, which she insisted had allowed her to keep her dignity throughout and left the department with her head held high.

Hopefully in the coming weeks her surgeon would correct those miserable, stress incontinence problems that had made her life so unbearable. And I had given no further thought to the proceedings in London. Thanks to Laura.

Christmas was approaching and Jeanette decided that the department should have an informal dinner to help new and old staff to get to know each other better, out of working hours. As usual she had struck the right chord as everyone including Mr. Petrie and Mavis eagerly agreed to participate.

Jeanette booked a small room in the oldest coaching inn in Elmbridge, where we would be served a Christmas style evening meal. The hotel manager kindly offered hospital staff, discount prices and lowered them even further for students.

As the evening drew near there was an air of excitement amongst us girls over what to wear and how to have our hair arranged, whereas Curtis and Mr. Petrie, the only men involved were very blasé about the whole affair. I had been really looking forward to the occasion and planned to dress up in my black mini-skirt and silver sparkly top to make a Christmassy splash, but when the evening arrived I felt inexplicably tired, sluggish even and rather reluctant to go.

"Are you Ok love? Mum asked, watching me closely with that over-bearing motherly concern which all young adults resented.

"Just a bit off, bit of a sore throat, I dunno, I'll be fine, don't worry," I replied trying to keep the edge from my voice. "And Curtis is dropping me home, he's borrowing his mother's new white Triumph Herald and can't wait to show off," I added hoping to change the subject from me.

"I hope he's careful, that's all," rejoined Mum now with something else to worry about. "Oh! His Mum'll kill him if he prangs it. He'll be careful alright!" I laughed.

Dad called up the stairs, "Are you ready yet Mary, I've got the car out?"

I grabbed my bag and dashed down to the open car and off we whizzed to town. I felt much better, chatting around, with a cold Babycham sparkling in my hand and waving the red glistening cocktail cherry on a stick, in the air, with the other. Soon we were seated and I was next to Collette, who kept me giggling throughout the meal over the different ways and stories of life in Northern

Ireland that beset a strictly brought up Catholic, Convent Schoolgirl. She seemed released by her freedom in England, no one to watch if she went to confession each day or attended mass twice a week or to judge how suitable each boy was that she talked to. Elmbridge was quite her idea of heaven.

As the evening passed along, I was aware that my voice became thicker and swallowing became more painful but I shrugged it off as one cigarette too many.

It was time to go, even Mr. Petrie had a seasonal glow about him, probably the wine, but it suited him and he looked relaxed and content as he glanced around the large table surrounded by all the x-ray staff, his staff, his department, success at last.

Clever Jeanette.

Curtis drove me home with the utmost care, enjoying the quiet hum of the Herald's engine and espousing its road holding qualities.

"Are you OK Mary?" he asked having suddenly glanced across at my unusually quiet demeanour, "You look really pale. Have you had too much to drink?"

"Oh come off it Curtis, I could only afford two Babychams, but no I feel quite odd, really not very well."

"Well here we are, get tucked up in bed. I'll see you Monday. Have a quiet weekend," he added as he helped me out from the car.

"Thanks for the lift, love the car. See you!" I called as I opened the front door and gratefully made my way to bed.

It was Sunday and Mum was worried. I had glands up everywhere with an accompanying high fever. "I'm calling the doctor!" she announced as she set off down the road to the telephone box.

He arrived, black bag in hand and cigarette clenched between his teeth, striding up the stairs to my bedroom. "Well young Mary, you do look a bit pale," he commented as he pushed a shaken thermometer under my tongue and closed my mouth around it, then felt all around my neck at the swollen glands. He took one look at the mercury level in the glass tube and pulled a face. 'Right, a bit on the high side so I am going to take a blood sample from your arm and we'll probably have a result by tomorrow," he added as he plunged the exposed needled syringe into the vein at my elbow.

"You're working in the x-ray department at Elmbridge General aren't you?" I nodded. "Two or three years now isn't it with radiation?" I nodded again and then oh dear it hit me, I knew where he was going with that information, I only hope Mum didn't.

"Right Mary, I'll see you tomorrow; afternoon probably. Stay where you are, aspirin for the fever and plenty of fluids."

He thinks I might have leukaemia my brain reported back to me, don't be so stupid I tried to reassure myself, you never take any risks, but the nasty thought kept creeping back and determinedly nagged at me all night long.

About three o'clock the following afternoon there was a fierce rattling at the front door.

As Mum opened it he came bounding up the stairs, grinning broadly, "Good news Mary, it's only glandular fever! No treatment, just carry on resting and it will run its course. I'll pop in later in the week just to check but you should be up and around by then, even if you still feel frail and tired. Mustn't get too used to bed!"

And lighting a fresh cigarette from the glowing butt of the last one he rushed off, leaving Mum wide-eyed that glandular fever could be considered good news especially after what had happened to James.

Mr. Petrie sent me back old Part Two examination questions, in all three subjects, so that I didn't fall behind with my studies, via Stella, who popped in regularly with the gossip and cheered me up every time she appeared to replace them with more.

Christmas came and went in a very subdued manner with just James coming for the two festive days. We settled happily back together, playing Totopoly, the horse racing board game produced by the manufactures of Monopoly and arguing companionably over our respective winnings. I missed him so much when he returned to London and became very miserable without his constant encouragement.

One afternoon about two weeks after Christmas there was loud laughter and quite a commotion outside the house. Mum opened the door to Joanna, Curtis and Linda, who streamed in on an absolute high.

"We passed, we all three passed!" exclaimed Joanna clapping her hands in excitement.

"Oh! Brilliant, that's the best news ever," I cried delightedly, "if you can all do it in six months I surely have to manage in twelve, don't I?" I asked anxiously looking at their beaming faces.

"Mary, no sweat, you're a cert!" agreed Curtis with a dreadful mock American accent.

"Sandra from Brunswick failed!" added Linda a trifle smugly, "Not on knowledge but on appearance. She went to the Viva Voce, oral exam on the second day wearing the shortest mini-skirt, heavily made-up with dark eyeliner and dangling from her ears were the hugest gold hooped earrings. Apparently the consultant radiologist examiner took one look at her and told her she was inappropriately dressed for the qualifying examinations of a medical professional and refused to ask her any questions. The superintendent radiographer examiner was a little kinder and tested her for the required fifteens minutes, but the damage was done; she now has to re-sit her oral exams, in April, when you take yours Mary."

"Come on you two, we're tiring the patient out," remonstrated Curtis seeing me yawn, "time to go."

They had reached the door when he suddenly turned back to me and took both my hands in his, then looking at me quite shyly, whispered, "Get better quickly, Mary, I really miss you!" then flashing his usual cheeky grin marched off to join the others waiting outside by the white Triumph Herald.

"What was all that about?" asked Mum who had seen everything from the top of the stairs.

"I have no idea," I replied, but as I spoke a glowing blush flooded my cheeks for all to see while I wondered what he had really meant by that.

"I'm going to lie down after all that excitement," I added rather shortly making my slow heavy steps up the stairs, but once in my bedroom I just sat on the edge of the bed feeling very light-headed and confused.

Chapter 23

I was in the queue, the long fidgety queue at Examination Hall, Queen's Square, nervously clutching my precious logbook, except this was not the queue for the hall it was the one for the loo! This was my third time in this loo queue trying to answer the thunderstorm currently erupting in my stomach.

Today was the second day of the Part Two examinations, the Viva Voce, when for half an hour each candidate was to be grilled for 15 minutes in turn, by a consultant radiologist and a superintendent radiographer. Army personnel had been seconded in to act the part of patients, so that we students could demonstrate the technical positioning for whichever part of the anatomy the examiners requested. One false move, one false response and that was that for another six months or so we believed.

I had, in a weird way, quite enjoyed yesterday's written papers, recognising one or two questions from the endless past papers that I had completed for Mr. Petrie whilst sick and the day had flown by.

Now, Sandra from Brunswick stood a little way ahead of me, we nodded and wished 'good-luck' to each other, but had no desire to chat. She was dressed modestly in grey and white. Her demure skirt fringed just below her knees and only the lightest touch of lipstick coloured her pale nervous complexion. She wore no jewellery of any kind and her natural nails were precise in their shape and length. She had learnt her lesson and was indeed a shining example of professionalism.

I had spent last night at Joanna's home to spare me the double trip to London, which gave her a chance to show me her new department, only a short walk away. She seemed to have settled in well and we enjoyed a giggly evening, reminiscing, catching up on the gossip.

"How's Curtis?" she asked with a meaningful glance at me.

"Just the same as ever, why?" I replied glancing sideways at her smirking face.

"Well don't know, thought you and he were getting a bit close," she laughed.

"Don't be daft, we're just good mates that's all," I retorted indignantly, but her comment unsettled me a little, until exam fever came back with a wallop and pushed it away. Joanna's company had made the evening tolerable but I spent an anxious, restless night. Tossing through my brain ran constant worries of how easy it was to correct a written answer, obliterate a written mistake as if it had never happened, but in the 'Viva' however I might try to rephrase a response, once any erroneous words had left my mouth a permanent impression would have been made. I dreaded the personal contact interrogation, far better to be an anonymous writer than a personified candidate.

Now finally here I was, positioned with my small group of students, in readiness for the next summons to an half an hour of hell!

The heavy double doors to the examination room swung open and twenty stark-eyed students emerged thankfully once more into the real world, while we were guided in to replace them. I was directed to a seemingly elderly gentleman, whose white, short-cropped hair topped a pince-nez perched studitiously on his beak-like nose.

He stood up and extended his hand to me, which I promptly took and shook, saying "Good morning."

"It was your logbook, not your hand I was seeking!" he replied sternly, looking at me with steely grey eyes.

'Damn, damn, damn,' I cursed inwardly, not a good start, still at least I was being polite!

He took the small, crammed and well thumbed book, beckoning me to sit down, while he quickly glanced through two and half years of hard work.

My initial responses to his questions seemed to satisfy him sufficiently for him to announce, "Now we shall move over to our patient so that you can position him as I request." He indicated a young soldier (the armed forces kindly provided 'mock patients' for examination purposes) of about eighteen years currently reclining on the nearby couch reading a paperback. This young man was dressed in khaki shorts and a T-shirt, bare legged, shoeless and sockless. He grinned up expectantly as we approached, stretching his long frame the full length of the couch.

"You must imagine that this young man has fallen and possibly fractured his left neck of femur, please proceed to x-ray him." I stood back and noted the exchange of humour between these two men. The consultant radiologist had requested a very nervous, fair skinned, fair-haired young woman to position this soldier's pelvis in such a way that his scrotum would be the main consideration. I felt sure they had this schemed together to cause me maximum embarrassment and watch amused, when my pale complexion turned gloriously red. One look at the soldier's smug expression confirmed that this nasty pair had set me up!

Well! I decided they were wrong. They were not going to make a fool of me I would be so cool and professional about this and resolutely summoned up all my self-control.

I calmly demonstrated the first straightforward view of the pelvis, placing gonad protection over the soldier's genitals with no hesitation and then came to the second more intimate position called 'the shoot-through lateral.'

I demonstrated placing an imaginary film against the soldier's left hip then instructed him to raise his right leg, which I took in my hand.

"I would support his uninjured leg up on a frame so that the main x-ray beam could be directed through his scrotum," as I aimed my pretend rays with my finger at the inner surface of his groin, in line with his neck of femur. "It is difficult to provide protection to the testicles in this view, because such lead screening could obscure the injured hip, but I would restrict the x-ray beam to its smallest applicable size thus reducing the more harmful and readily absorbed, soft scattered radiation," I concluded in a cool, business like manner, my skin retaining its for once wonderful pallor, then turned around to look coldly at the examiner, who could surely hear the fierce hammering of my heart resonating beneath my blouse. But I knew I had positioned the soldier correctly and more importantly, for my own self-respect, I had thwarted their attempts to embarrass me. I felt elated I had won!

"Relax soldier, we're finished here," the radiologist instructed, just as the change-over bell summoned me on to the superintendent radiographer, for the remaining fifteen minutes.

He was charming and in total contrast tried to put me at my ease. I answered all his questions with confidence and at the end of the allotted time walked out of that room with my head held high. My Viva Voce had gone better than I dared hope.

It was over!

The re-telling of my encounter with the soldier greatly amused all the other radiographers especially as they knew how awkward I would have felt and the crimson shade my face was capable of acquiring.

"Well done Mary," smiled Jeanette, "just shows how strong you can be, which must have boosted your confidence no end. Now, I have to have a chat with you later, so can you meet me in the sitting room at lunchtime? Good I'll see you then."

I sat waiting in the still quietness of the radiographers' sitting room, pondering that Jeanette might not have very good news, as the door opened.

"Oh good you're here already," Jeanette exclaimed as she sat in the armchair opposite me. "What are you hoping to do, career wise, once you have qualified?" she asked.

"Well, rather like Curtis and Linda I hope to stay on for a while to gain experience, especially in 'on-call' work, but I imagine you're going to say the department is now fully staffed and I shall have to move on…. that is…. if I pass this time round."

"Certainly staff numbers are a concern we have, but we really don't want to lose you, you've grown up with us, however unfortunately sentiment doesn't create jobs. Still don't do anything hasty until your results are through; I will explore all the options and we'll talk again later. Don't look so worried," she added, "you need your Diploma first before any decisions are made."

Curtis caught up with me as I walked back along the corridor seriously deep in thought.

"Do you fancy a drink tonight to celebrate surviving Part Two Viva?"

"That would be lovely. I could do with going out tonight, away from parents' question time! Can you pick me up?"

"Well that was the intention, 7.30 pm suit?" he asked.

"Yeah fine I'll see you then," I replied feeling his support.

On my home it suddenly struck me, had Curtis asked me out as a friend, ex-fellow student, pal, mate etc. or crumbs, after Joanna's strange comment, what if it was a date?

I wasn't sure anymore, there had been that equally strange moment when I was ill, that 'he'd missed me', but he delighted in teasing me and winding me up, joking and joshing and sharing cigarettes and funny stories. What was going on? Perhaps after all I could use the wisdom of a parent, I would ask Mum.

We sat on the edge of her bed as I confided my uncertainty about Curtis's invitation.

"Dear, I think he is very fond of you, he definitely gave me that impression when they all called in here. How do you feel if it's more than just mates having a drink but a date instead?" she enquired.

"I've never considered he might be interested in me so I've no idea. I like him very much, we've shared a lot over the past two years, but he fools around and I'm frightened of being made to look stupid."

"No, Mary," Mum insisted, "Curtis would never be unkind like that. Why don't you see how it goes tonight, for I'm sure you will have a better idea by the end of the evening? Be yourself, enjoy yourself, you deserve a break after all these long weeks of studying."

For whatever reason, suddenly I wanted to look my best, so I decided to wear my favourite black watch tartan, mini-kilt and a powder blue jumper that showed off my flicked out, freshly washed and gleaming, shoulder length, fair hair. I was just putting on a brown suede jacket when Mum showed Curtis into the lounge.

"You look nice Mary," he smiled, quite shyly, "shall we go to the local pub it shouldn't be too crowded there?"

We found a table in the corner and were soon chatting away in our usual relaxed manner, when all at once he reached across and took my hand.

"Were you surprised when I asked you out for a drink?" he asked quietly.

"No not really, not until I suddenly wondered..... Curtis why did you?" I asked, all in a rush, blushing madly.

"I've wanted to ask you out for sometime, but while we were both students it could have made life difficult especially for Linda and Joanna, but now I'm qualified and you are nearly too, I thought I'd pluck up the courage today, especially as you looked pretty down this afternoon after your meeting with Jeanette."

"You, pluck-up courage to ask me? You've spent two and a half years teasing and winding me up.... I can't believe you worried about asking me." I answered in amazement.

"I didn't know what your reaction would be. I hoped maybe we could find out if we liked each other more than just mates because I really like you Mary, it's whether you might get to like me," he concluded looking rather wistful and uncertain, then added, "perhaps we could go out a few times and see what happens?"

"Yes I would like that, but no one in the department must know, else the hospital grapevine will have us married off by next week," I insisted.

He drove me home and gave me a very chaste kiss on the cheek. "Do you fancy the pictures on Friday?"

"That would be lovely. I'll see you at work tomorrow but not a word!" I insisted.

Mum was of course still waiting up, eager to learn what had happened.

"Goodnight dear." Then, "How did it go?" added as if by casual afterthought.

"Goodnight Mum, Oh! It went OK. By the way it was a date and we're off to the pictures Friday," I added, seeing my smiling face reflected in the mirror as I closed my bedroom door.

We managed to keep our dating under wraps for about a month, then one night in a village pub some miles outside Elmbridge, Dr. Weston Smythe strolled in with a group of friends. He took one look around for a table and spotted us immediately.

"Hello, hello have I stumbled across a secret liaison," he chortled, as he made his way over to us, "Sorry but this is too good to keep to myself; I always thought you two went well together," and moved off still chuckling, to join his own party.

"That's blown it, he's bound to tell Doreen and then it'll be all around the department!" I exclaimed quite crossly.

"We've had a good run," Curtis chided, "and we are still going out, perhaps he's right, perhaps we do go well together, what do you think?"

This time I leant across the table for a proper kiss and agreed we had to face the department tomorrow as a couple.

The postman delivered a cardboard tube, heavily sealed at each end and asked for my signature as recipient. I ripped it open with huge grin, knowing from the others that rolled inside was my long awaited official certification to become a proud owner of the Diploma of the Society of Radiographers, along with its accompanying letter of congratulations, and the more mundane forms to complete for State Registration.

I was now, finally, a fully qualified radiographer; the little five year old girl had realised her dreams but, and of course there is always a "but", was there a job for me would I be employed?

Everyone in the department seemed delighted by my success.

"I bet Mrs. L is looking down smiling on yer!" grinned Stella.

"I'll let Ted know," beamed Connie.

Linda nudged me, "Make sure you tell Joanna, Mary" she insisted.

"Does anyone know how to contact Elizabeth?" asked Brenda.

Mr. Petrie nodded, "I'll pass on your good news when we send her back her notes," he agreed, delighted to achieved 100% pass rate with his first full complement of students; it was an equally proud moment for him.

Doreen emerged from her office adding her and Judy's pleasure at my news, then said, "Mary, Dr. Weston Smythe wants to see you."

"Fine I'll come straight away," I replied alight with my success.

Dr. Weston Smythe rose from his desk and took my hand, "Well done Mary, not only have you passed these papers but in every subject including the Viva Voce you have gained distinction. We are extremely proud of you and certainly don't want to lose such an illustrious student. Sit down and I will explain what the Management Committee and I have agreed to."

It was all rather overwhelming. I couldn't believe I had done that well, but the Society sent every student's marks back to their school so he must be right.

"We have a part-time position vacant in this department, two and a half days a week, which we can marry up with two and a half empty days at the geriatric hospital. Now, I know that is not ideal but you would take your turn on the 'on-call' roster here, that is one evening a week and one weekend in six, sharing some duties in the longer Bank Holiday weekends, which will give you the experience you particularly wanted. Go away and think about it carefully and let me know tomorrow. It is the best we can do, but also in light of your recent relationship with Curtis perhaps you two shouldn't be working quite so closely together now. Talk it over at home, consider all the factors." He got up and shook my hand in dismissal, "Well done Mary, very well done!" and I left his office, his praise ringing in my ears.

Chapter 24

It was Whitsun Bank Holiday and the first weekend that I was involved with 'on-call'. My spell of duty spanned from 12.30 p.m. Saturday until 9.00 a.m. Monday, when Mr. Petrie was scheduled to take over the remaining hours until the department fully re-opened at 9.00 o'clock Tuesday morning.

Curtis had worked with me both Saturday and Sunday up until 10.00 p.m., helping me to adjust to the pressures of becoming radiographer, receptionist, darkroom technician and film finder. The duties seemed endless. The weekend had been busy with minor injuries and acute medical conditions. Saturday night, just about mid-night, I had been brought in from home by the duty driver to x-ray a patient in excruciating pain caused by a possible bowel obstruction. The films had confirmed that diagnosis so I had returned home satisfied by my competence.

Then Sunday, in the middle of the night at 3.00 a.m., I had been called in for an emergency admission of a patient in heart failure and performed a satisfactory chest x-ray, all of which boosted my confidence. The night driver returned me home once more to bed, where amazingly I fell straight back to sleep.

Early next morning at seven o'clock, once more the telephone shrilled into action, its harsh tone clanging in my head, making me quickly yank off the receiver.

" There is an emergency in casualty but the night driver is on another mission so one of the night nurses' boyfriends is coming to pick you up," announced the switchboard operator, "he apparently knows you and where you live," she added before ringing off.

I threw on my white coat and secured it with its new bright red belt of qualification anchored by a beautiful silver buckle that Curtis mother had given me from her days as a nursing sister. I drew back the curtains to see a jazzy little red sports car pull up outside. I rushed out to be greeted by an old friend from church youth club, whose current girl friend, a theatre staff nurse, he had been off to collect from finishing her night duty.

"Hop in Mary, you have a right one to deal with," he exclaimed, " old boy shot half his face off with a twelve bore shot gun. Tried to commit suicide but didn't quite succeed," he added with relish.

"Oh! Robert you're having me on!" I laughed.

"No truly, you'll soon see, nasty this is!" he exclaimed eyebrows raised in warning.

With no traffic to impede us we were at the hospital within a few minutes. I rushed down to the x-ray department to switch all the equipment on so that it could be warming up while I went to casualty to find out the truth.

There carefully positioned on the special x-ray trolley, lay a motionless patient with the right side of his head concealed beneath swathes of bandages.

I grabbed the x-ray request form and realised that Robert not been joking as I scanned down to read the following list: skull, facial bones and mandible views, all tricky films at the best of times but incredibly difficult on a patient with much of those areas missing.

The two porters accompanied by a staff-nurse wheeled the old man down the long corridor and into the general x-ray room.

We steadied the trolley and braked it under the x-ray camera as I steeled myself to ask the nurse, "Please remove all the bandages so that I can see where and how to position my films."

Moments later we were staring into a huge gaping hole in his skull, streams of blood congealing around the wound but some still seeping over what remained of his face. Somehow I had to deal with the horror of this situation in order to assess it technically. It meant that I had to concentrate solely on adapting every textbook position into what was achievable.

I rushed busily from side to side, balanced cassettes in precarious positions, angled the x-ray tube in unknown planes, took the requested shots as far as was possible, to produce diagnostic images and with those to hand, as quickly as I could returned this desperately, self-injured man to casualty. The day shift duty driver collected me as I finished closing down the department and returned me home, where, starving hungry I devoured one of Mum's full English breakfasts.

At 9.15 a.m. the phone sprang to life once more as Mum summoned me over to take the call. "Mary," came Mr. Petrie's stern, unhesitating voice, "it's about your shotgun patient."

"Yes," I replied half expecting to be congratulated on the results I had managed to achieve. "Where is his chest x-ray?" he asked curtly.

"Chest film?" I queried. "No, they didn't ask for a chest x-ray, just skull and facial and mandible bone series," I replied with certainty.

"Well I'm looking at the request form now, in my hand, and it has written at the top in capitals CXR!" he stated fiercely (the medical short-hand for chest x-ray)

"Oh! I am so sorry, I missed that!" I cried in horrified frustration. After all my careful work I had failed!

Mr. Petrie had been summoned in to make good my error but by the time he arrived the patient had got his wish and died, leaving the casualty doctor to determine whether that missing film would have made any difference to the old man's probable inevitable and greatly desired death. My first 'on-call' had ended in shame.

After nearly three years there still remained so much for me to learn. I was starting again at the very bottom.

Printed in Great Britain
by Amazon